# The FEBRUARY Novel

## Written By

## Erica S. Elliott

ARNICA PRESS

Published by ARNICA PRESS

www.ArnicaPress.com

Copyright © 2021 Erica S. Elliott

Cover Art by Erica S. Elliott

www.EricaSwensonElliott.com

Printed in the United States of America.

ISBN: 978-1-7352446-8-6

Book Two

## BY ERICA SWENSON ELLIOTT

### LOVE & TAXES SERIES
*Love & Taxes*
*Love & Business*

### AMERICA'S REMARKABLE HOMES
*The Dunrobin Castle*

### THE CALENDAR NOVELS SERIES

*The January Novel*

*The February Novel*

*The March Novel*

### THE CALENDAR NOVELS
*A collection of stories about the mystical journey of souls transcending space and time. Each book is a delicious morsel that can be savored independent of the others. However, we humans do enjoy the comfort of our linear timelines. Therefore, you may enjoy the more traditional chronological journey wandering through one calendar day at a time. Onward we go!*

*Sweet Keith,*

*Do you ever get the feeling*

*that whatever we are doing here*

*is more important than it appears?*

*Are we somehow shaping a future outcome?*

*What if we are foreshadowing our future selves?*

*Wherever you may be next time, I will come find you again.*

*But I promise I will not make you wait so long.*

*All my love,*

*Erica*

# TABLE OF CONTENTS

# BRAVING THE JOURNEY

*45°42'48.9"N 75°16'57.3"W*
*North American upper plains, 2500s*

A vaporous mist hovered over the frozen grasses dotting the tundra. The temperature crept upwards, releasing water from its frozen state into the air. The rolling plain stretched as far as the young man could see. Despite the overwhelming feeling of solitude evoked by this blank canvas, he continued to softly walk across the great expanse.

His tribal leader's directions rang in his ears:
"Walk East towards the great waters of what was once called the Atlantic. Walk toward the rising sun and moon for at least one full moon cycle. Once you reach the ocean, turn South, until you reach a grouping of islands. You will eventually find the island we seek. It is the Island of the Lady."

He asked, "But how am I to know that it is the right island?"

His elder replied, "The legends ring true. There is no mistaking this place. For when you arrive you will meet the Lady face to face, and there will be no mistaking her for any other. But rest assured, for we taught you to speak and read their old English letters for this very mission. You may find a few ancient road signs that will help you. You may ask for directions, but be careful whom you ask, for you will be a stranger among them."

As the young man pondered these words, his fingers reached for the burden that he carried over his heart. The mysterious foreign object snugly fit in the small leather pouch, that securely hung from sturdy twine, hand-strung by their village's tanner.

The most distressing aspect of this journey was his last conversation which occurred the morning of his departure.

The young man had already said his personal goodbyes to his family. Now he faced the same ancient village elder, who stood teetering in the wind. His wrinkled wizened face finely polished by a life lived on the windy plains. His piercing eyes set as permanent crescents beneath craggy brows. Yet these physical frailties seemed only to highlight the powerful soul force emanating from their leader. The young man stood mute in subdued awe, thinking upon the fact that this man had probably lived four of his own lifetimes already. And in these primitive times, no one lived that long. If it was not a violent accident, or a human battle, it was a plague.

Suddenly, the elder said with a terrible severity, "From this day forward your name is Brave. We have been waiting for you to come through us since the days of my father's father. For it has been in our history that our tribe will send the Messenger forth. The proper time only known when the Messenger is revealed and clearly understood."

Quietly he paused. The tip of his tongue wetted his cracked lips, seeming to give him courage to carry on. "You are the Messenger. Since you were born, you affirmed that you were the bravest young man our village had seen." Assembling a small, smile he again paused and said, "Not that bravery is always paired with intelligence, as one must often be stupid to perform brave acts."

A hawk screamed overhead as it circled the small village looking for a meal.

With no small consternation, the young man fell to his knees in front of his elder, humbled by this tart assessment of his young life's athletic prowess. To this point he was proud of being selected for this mysterious mission as their Messenger. But now all his sporting achievements seemed juvenile. The fear of the unknown awoke in his belly, unsettling his steely nerves even more.

Brave whispered, "What am I to do?"

And then the shocking missive, "You must bring the object to the Island of the Lady. The Lady will have her own agent, whom you must work with closely. It will become your joint mission to unlock its mysteries."

Brave was struck almost dumb. This was way beyond his abilities. He enjoyed winning the youthful competitions of wind sprints and up-river swims, when the simple objective was to win. But this was different, he did not even know the actual goal. What object? What mystery?

Suddenly, his elder brought forth the leather pouch. Solemnly he said, "This is a key to our past and therefore our future. It explains much that we have lost, but it needs the right people and processes applied. It was our job to keep it safe until the right time."

Again, with that intimidating pause, he licked his lips again before he continued, "And the time is now, for you are definitely the Messenger. Take it. Trust those of the Island of the Lady for they also hold some of the keys to unlock the mystery of our futures.

# MEDLEY OF THOUGHTS

*39.7447° N, 75.5484° W*
*Wilmington, Delaware, 2000s*

Sean was comfortable at his home away from home. He was ensconced in his latest corporate office. He was a great clean up - fix up kind of CFO. A lone wolf of sorts. More times than not he would get the call from a company struggling to make the magic number so they could qualify for acquisition at the proper price. They had a great product or process for sale. But as he would often say, most corporate officers were one trick ponies. Once their favorite idea ran its course, they were fresh out of new tricks. If they knew how to grow revenue, then often they did not know how to manage costs. That is where Sean would come in and remedy their weaknesses, which often was a painful process. The bearer of bad news was not always viewed as a friend. But eventually the company and its financial statements were better prepared for a sale. But often Sean's solutions were painful to implement, so quite often the only thanks Sean received was in his bonus check. Even upon the business owners' newly forged financial success, they were happy enough to see Sean's back.

But today he had a pain in his shoulder, which distracted him from the trial balance at hand. His internal dialogue was a layered medley of thoughts.

"All those years of swimming the breaststroke in college is catching up with me...if their inventory numbers could be brought more into alignment with their industry norms...it must be bursitis...it better not affect my golf swing! I just figured out how to hit that sand flop shot...maybe if I can get ahold of the Atlanta plant manager this weekend to better understand that big shift...wonder if Janice can come and stay with me for a longer time this month..."

Life as a corporate road warrior was not easy, especially in one's home life. Sean's first marriage had not survived it. But with Janice it was totally different. Since the moment they met they were allies. Sean did not believe all that mumbo jumbo of past life stuff. Yet if anything would make him a believer it was when he looked into her eyes. It was so strange or as his Jewish friends would say, it was kismet. That first meeting was as if they had known each other forever. Now that they were reunited, they were just filling in the blanks. There was no need "to work on their relationship" as described in the common vernacular. They just belonged together.

Even when Janice was sick, it did not come between them. They always figured things out as they went along. Sean took to the road to perform his corporate duties. When she could join him, she did, and it was magic all over again.

They shared a lot of common business interests and enjoyed a daily meeting of the minds. No matter where they were in the world, if they were together, they would put responsibilities aside and rehash the puzzles of the day at their own cocktail hour. But their physical attraction was just as strong as their mental magnetism. Or maybe one fueled the other.

It was her powerful legs that rocked his world when he first laid eyes on her. To watch her walking away from him that first time left a palpable lump in his throat, for her rear view was more lovely than the front, if that was even possible...

By now Sean had completely forgotten the financials spread out before him as his mind wandered away to that very first night together. Reliving each magical moment.

# DREAMING THE IN BETWEEN

*45.4042° N, 71.8929° W*
*North American great plains, 2500s*

B rave looked up into the heavens above him, as he settled down for another night on the open plains. He tried to imagine what it must have been like long ago, the stories about cities shining so bright through the night, that one could not see the stars shining anymore. That seemed impossible to believe really, for the darkness was like black velvet wrapped around him.

He saw the waning moon beginning to rise in the East, as his eyes finally grew drowsy. Another few days, and he should find the big ocean. He had never seen the big waters, so his curiosity certainly peaked. But he could sense the air was changing, there was more humidity than what he was used to in his nomadic life on the arid plains. But it had something else in it. Salt? It was an odd mix, the humid air felt heavy in his lungs. But his lips seemed to be dried as when they over salted the venison.

As Brave descended into sleep, strange people and places began to appear in his mind. None of which he had ever seen before.  Smooth surfaces on the ground and many square boxes where people lived inside of them with nothing living around them.  Everything was cold, dead metals and some clear process called glass...then the dream took him deeper and deeper leaving his conscious mind floating far above him like a tiny sailboat on the surface of the ocean.

# WEAVING THE TAPESTRY

*The Space In Between Time*

Darius stood with his Indigo blue cape swirling around him, as he leaned forwards over the mystical tapestry. His shoulders curved over his outstretched arms. His brows furrowed deep in thought as his long fingers curved around the edges of the ever-growing tapestry.

It was not made from material as it was in the spaces betwixt and between the physical. But it was alive. For this was a real symbol, well as much as something can be tangible in the spirit world. At the very least it represented the very real lives that were being lived in the murky mire of the real.

And like all woven things, it is made of threads, but each thread represents a soul. Each soul lived a physical life, or sometimes numerous lives. And if one could follow the tangled web, the Tapestry was a map of future possibilities. Not many souls could follow the twisted paths, for it took patience and understanding. Here in the spirit world, there were many masters of numerous specialties. But there were few that had mastered the messages woven into the Tapestry. And of the few, there was only one Darius.

He had lived countless lives on Earth and other places. So much so, he no longer had lessons to learn in the physical. Long ago, Darius had finished with that part of his soul's growth. For at least an aeon he had now remained in the spirit world, where he applied the layers of his skills to the souls still journeying through the clay.

Clay is what the spirits called the physical body. A quaint term named for the proverbial dust to dust. At this juncture, Darius' eyes were locked on numerous vibrating threads, under the weavers' gentle touch. There were a few junctures wandering off in ever widening positions. The Tapestry was not a pre-destination tool. It was more a tool to understand the hypotheticals, a term devised by some of the younger souls.

It was predictive of future outcomes; it did not set what was about to occur. It required a master's touch like Darius for with one misstep it could open and close multiple timelines or outcomes for one event.

Based on Darius' deepening frown, it could not be predicting anything of great joy. If one followed Darius' sorrowful gaze, there were frazzled ends leaping from the frame, almost like electricity bolting through the air. One of the weaver's paused and asked Darius if he would enjoy a brief respite of refreshment. With an engrossed shrug, Darius spun about and disappeared in a crack of red sparks. Gone without a trace.

After recovering from the shock of Darius' unusually abrupt departure, the cherubic weaver returned to her work. Over the course of her commitment to the Tapestry, she had grown accustomed to Darius' unexpected appearances and departures. He was like a nutty professor coming and going without introductions, wandering the campus deep in thought.

One could easily be quite forgiving after reading the tales of Darius' brave and ingenious deductions in the Spirit Library. He was pondering big burdens that few shoulders could carry, even here on the other side. And it was not until centuries later when his adventures were recorded that it became clear what a solitary road Darius often traveled. He was hacking a way through the mire for the spirit and human worlds to follow. Not always but sometimes, he was the only lantern lighting the way for others to follow.

# BRINY BREEZES

*45.2733° N, 66.0633° W*
*The upper reaches of the Atlantic Ocean, 2500s*

Now Brave felt the full flush of sea spray for the very first time. It seemed magical that salt could be carried in the air like this. Salt was something scarce and difficult to come by in their tribe's life on the plains. It was a resource that they sometimes physically craved. As he stood with his bare feet in the roaring surf of the ocean, he never felt so alive. This was so unlike the great lakes of the plains, murky, deep, and still. His senses were in overload, for no one alive in his community today had any concept of the scale and movement of an ocean. And certainly, none of them could imagine having salt encrusted eyelashes! It was a magical gift from nature!

Completely alone with the sea, suddenly Brave was so enamored he sprinted towards the waves dove into the wild surf. He finished his afternoon with a cavorting run along the shoreline, in a childlike attempt to mimic the sandpipers' dance with the tides.

As the day wound down, he grew more solemn as he built a small driftwood fire on the beach to cook his dinner of small game. For all his joy from seeing the ocean for the first time, there was a dark foreboding in the pit of his stomach.

He still did not fully understand the mechanics of his mission. But he understood that it was serious. He did not know that his tribe had been guarding lost knowledge for generations, until he was summoned that day. What was this knowledge that they protected?

From stories told, he knew that there used to be a great global civilization a long time ago. There had been great stone urban centers with tall, tall buildings. Funnily, they had named these skyscrapers. In their arrogance, they thought they could reach the skies, apparently. They had magicians that could turn metal into amazing tools like flying and driving machines.

But the most mysterious invention of their ancestors' inventions was invisible. Somehow, they built a vast web to hold human knowledge, like a library built out of thin air. Apparently, they had so much knowledge, there were not enough books in a physical library to hold it all, so they built this invisible one. Or maybe it was to protect it from their enemies? Hide it? But what if they lost the magic key to access it?

But these sophisticated ancestors were decimated a long time ago. After their near mass extinction, their beautiful cities stood empty for a time. Within a hundred years or so, the tumbled skyscrapers crumbled slowly as they were clawed back by Nature. Eventually they disappeared back into the wilds that existed long before them.

According to the legends, the cause was really a combination of multiple human and natural actions. It was a perfect storm of cataclysmic events that decimated billions of their ancestors, leaving only a remnant of humanity to crawl back out of the abyss.

One part was a surprise deluge of meteors that entered the Earth's atmosphere, all along the belt of humanity living along the Earth's bulging middle. These caused massive tidal waves wiping out entire coastal cities across the globe.

Somehow, this triggered active supervolcanoes circling the globe too. Maybe it was the seismic disruption by each asteroid's impact? Their resulting massive ash clouds created deep changes in the weather patterns that destroyed crops for years to come.

Then the volcanos' swirling ash clouds contributed to the spread of reactivated ancient plagues. The survivors in the world's bread belt, were now almost all gone. The Remnant left the middle wasteland for the more stable zones closer to the two poles.

After some time, these fringes of civilization found some stability for sustainable life. All the scientists were gone now, their sparkling laboratories lost in the global mass destruction. So, experience and intuition again became the primary tools for deductive reasoning. Therefore, the survivors came to believe that the re-activated plague viruses preferred the hot weather along the equator where most of their ancestors had once lived. They came to believe that they could better ensure humanity's survival if they remained in the cooler climates. They also felt it was safer if they separated into tribes, so they would not cross-contaminate each other with latent retroviruses.

They half believed the stories of their distant past, that the Earth had once cared for over 6 billion humans at one time. But that seemed quite impossible to comprehend. Brave had only laid eyes on one hundred humans in his lifetime. And that sometimes was too many people to be around!

There used to be many books made of something called paper. But the process of making paper was now lost after the massive near extinction. Brave had only seen three books one time. They were venerated as sacred objects kept at his tribal leader's home. However, the pages were so delicate and ancient now, they were mostly kept tucked away in a desperate attempt at preservation in their primitive life.

This sparse library was the source of Brave's written language lessons. It had been rough going, but he eventually had mastered every word found in those books. Mind you, he only worked from copies, for the originals would almost disintegrate upon touch. He would practice his letters with alternative resources. Sometimes, he would scratch with a quill on an animal's hide, or trace words in the sand.

Today the Earth was a harsh environment where to live. It was a matter of survival. The human race's meager remains coalesced their ingenuity now on finding sustenance.

There was a valid concern there were not enough people left to continue the race. After hundreds of years in their self-imposed tribal quarantines, the gene pools were getting too narrow. Babies were beginning to be born with severe defects. It was getting to the place, where tribal leaders realized they would need to find and reconnect with other people groups, before it was too late.

Another legend was from a more recent time period: it was about the Twelve. About one hundred years ago, there were one dozen surviving leaders from within the plague infested humanity belt. They were immensely powerful spiritual beings. They were connected to The Source more so than others. Perhaps because they practiced listening to that inner small voice.

Each of the Twelve were scholars of the lost human history. They dedicated their lives to recording, retaining, and learning as much they could from the past. To protect the knowledge from further destruction, the Twelve had spread themselves out in the great diaspora, attaching each of themselves to a different people group.

They had knowledge of humans' many past abuses of power. For example, governments had manipulated weather patterns to scare and control the masses. Others had scientifically created plagues through laboratory mutations. Then they offered medical solutions to combat the diseases they created for a contrived profit. Their intentions were to combat disease, but they did not really understand the multi-dimensional complexity of what they were experimenting with. How could they? They were operating in the third-dimensional reality where they lived.

Driven by the lust for more power, they turned a blind eye to their indirect contribution to the cataclysmic events. They chose to ignore the possible catastrophic outcomes of their manipulations. Then the mutations took on a life of their own, that were beyond the scientists' control.

Based on these past horrific outcomes, The Twelve did not trust the remaining humans to purify their motives. They felt the need for continued intervention. Instead of continuing to rely on their meetings of their minds, they decided to physically come together one more time to preserve knowledge for the protection of the future of humanity. They needed to create a physical backup in essence. Just in case others could not access the space in between where all the knowledge was eternally stored like the Twelve could.

They met in the ancient hills of the Cherokee nation where the air was still clear. Using their superior ingenuity, they somehow downloaded swaths of all-important knowledge from this library in the air before virtual access to this invisible knowledge base was shut down for good. They placed some of the keys into twelve physical objects for safekeeping. Each leader was responsible for one of these vessels.

They wanted to save it for a future society so they would have a handbook of all their learning. But they did not want it all in one place, for they did not want the lust for domination to destroy humanity all over again. So, they each took only a portion of the knowledge keys with them, and then they fled to the corners of the Earth.

# SPINNING

*39.7447° N, 75.5484° W*
*Wilmington, Delaware, 2000s*

Now it was February, and they were approaching his birthday again. Sean wanted to be with her to celebrate their new-found life together.

He took off his platinum wedding band that was a Rolex-type basket weave. Then from his right, he removed the gold signet college ring that was showing some wear and tear. As his thoughts drifted towards travel logistics, he idly began to spin the signet ring like an upside-down top on the lacquered wooden desk.

He wanted to take Janice to New York City for his birthday weekend. She would have to fly up from their home in Florida, but he could take the train up and meet her in The Big Apple. He wanted Janice to see some of the unexpected art he had unsurfaced there.

Nimbly, his mind moved from topic to topic as he searched for personal and corporate solutions. Blindly, he gazed through the glass walls that ran from floor to ceiling, into the tangle of woods which clung to the banks of the Brandywine River, despite the surrounding urban infringements.

Of all the places he had worked, this one felt most like home. Perhaps it was because his first career opportunity post MBA was here in Wilmington, Delaware. Maybe it was a coming home scenario.

But it was not just his career, it was the Brandywine artists that spoke to his soul. During his first stop in Wilmington, he was too worried about making the grade and paying the bills to seriously consider collecting art.

As he twirled his signet ring, his mind returned to that distant sunlit Saturday outdoor market, where he first met Andrew Wyeth. Drenched in that morning's sunbeams, the oil paintings' bucolic realistic scenes glistened. His eye followed the haphazard line of works draped over the meandering fence line. At that time in Sean's young professional life, one of the artist's paintings equaled one year of his mortgage payments. But today, he could trade one of the great artist's paintings for a city block. Sean shook his head in regretful bemusement.

However, returning to today, Sean's heart leapt with joy as he thought of his current ability to be a Patron of the Arts. Particularly, he was proud of the art competition he helped the company start for young high school students in the state. This is what mattered most to him:  using corporate and personal means to provide opportunities for youth to make inspiring art. Subconsciously, he also knew that when individuals created things, they were healthy.  Probably because they were built in the image of their Source that built them all.

Like many with a gruff exterior, a sensitive soul lived inside.  Sean was not sure why, but somewhere deep down in his DNA layers, his artful passion burned like an eternal flame.

# MAKING AN IMPRESSION

*48.8566° N, 2.3522° E*
*Paris, France, 1870s*

M onsieur Durand-Ruel, stroked the thick mustaches that descended over the corners of his mouth, which created an artificial frown line. This despite the small smile creeping across his face, safely hidden beneath each blonde whisker.

The object of his amusement was his hosts' young, awkward daughter trudging down the stairs of their fashionable Parisian townhome. It was as if she was approaching her imminent death at the guillotine of the long-ago French Revolution instead of a dinner party. She was a shy child, as she could barely make small talk with him as expected of young ladies of the day.

Mademoiselle Janette's mother watched with a judgmental eye her daughter's awkward lack of charming etiquette with their guest. But as the Laurent dinner progressed around their dinner table, something shifted. Monsieur Duran-Ruel began to speak to Monsieur Laurent, about an interesting transaction in his business as an art dealer. As his tale unwound about the shift of his interest from the Barbizon School of artists to the avant-garde Impressionists, Janette began to tremble as if she was a leaf in the wind.

Like a gunshot, the young woman bounded straight out of her chair, standing ramrod straight at her place at the table. If one was only a fly on the wall, it would be quite amusing to observe the abject terror on her Mother's face, when she realized that all sensibility had been lost. One could see the thoughts marching across her eyes from shock to complete self-repudiation for letting her offspring be seen by an outsider. But as a sensitive sort, Monsieur Durand-Ruel's empathy went out to the poor duo of mother and daughter locked in this eternal drama.

With a tremor in her voice, the young woman spoke quite loudly. This was probably perceived as more loudly than it really was, if only because of the contrast to the poor wretch's absolute silence throughout the meal.

"Oui ! Monsieur Durand-Ruel ! The Impressionnistes ! Please tell me ALL you know! I have heard so much but seen not one! I paint, I paint what is in my heart and my mind. But they are inspired by nature! They paint en plein air. And alas I paint in my garret for I am a young woman and that would not appear seemly…"

And with that the poor soul's speech sputtered to its pitiful end. The child sat down silent staring aimlessly out into the hallway while she twirled her fork between her fingers like a paintbrush.

There was now a painful stretch of silence that the kindly businessman broke with a quick clap of his hands as he brought them together almost in a brief supposition of prayer.

"Come, come! I must see one of these garret paintings! Art must first be seen if it is ever to be admired! Art may be made among the rafters, but it must not remain there into perpetuity!"

Now the art dealer's voice was deep as a foghorn at sea and it practically made the glassware vibrate. With a clatter of footsteps, one could hear the shocked countryside maids scampering up the stairs to meet this unexpected demand from their Mistress' house guest.

And suddenly in a jumble, three of Janette's paintings were aligned in the arms of housemaids. With a start, the art dealer stood as well, with his arms folded across his broad chest, as he stared with his mouth beginning to gape. For here were three paintings in the same vein as the emerging Impressionist art of the men forging a new path. How was this possible? For clearly this young girl was not participating in the salons or attending the exhibitions. She said so herself. She could barely function at her family's table.

Monsieur had been forming a theory from an intuition of his after dealing with artists over the years. There must be some idea floating in the air that was available for the soul that could see it or hear it. There had been a few times, where the concept or technique had been repeated by artists unknown to each other. But never like this. This was a woman-child, and she was using some of the rebellious non-conforming brushstrokes, in complete isolation. There was no undue influence.

It confirmed his personal feeling that this was the awakening of a new movement away from the formal dark paintings of historical scenes and portraiture.

What was this? It was something beyond art. It was some powerful source or being that was speaking through random strangers. Monsieur shook his head one more time to clear his thoughts and he began to speak:

"Monsieur Laurent, this is quite unusual a request I know. But these are unusual times. Mademoiselle is quite unique, for somehow through her own volition she is independently practicing the techniques of these new artists of which we were just speaking. As we all know, any woman's work will not be taken seriously. But if you will allow," here he paused and bowed his head, "I will take these works by Janette. We will exhibit them under a man's pseudonym, so no one will discover her identity, to protect her character. And above all else, she must keep painting."

With that shocking pronouncement, Monsieur bowed deeply over her hand, as Janette whispered, "I see pictures in my mind, they speak to me and they demand expression."

# DREAM STATE

*The Space In Between Time*

In the great space between the stars, Darius' spirit mimicked the human form of one deep in thought. His cloak swirled about his ankles as he paced to and fro, his chin sunk down deeply into his chest, so the wisps of his gray beard dangled almost to his belt.

It was difficult working in two time periods on Earth. For here in the Spirit world, there was no linear time there was only eternity. However, when a spirit entered a physical world, it got very murky. It was like a person trying to open their eyes under water, nothing was as it appeared.

Brave's spirit was known by the nickname Shev, short for Shevanon. Jokingly, his soul group often called him Shove, because he shoved so much into every life that he lived.

During the 1870's in Paris, he lived the pivotal life of Paul Durand-Ruel, the great patron of the Impressionist movement. He helped influence the dramatic shifts of that time. Then in the 2000's, Shev, or Shove, lived the life of Sean the hard charging corporate executive with a heart for the arts. Now here was Shev again shoving all the previous lessons learned into the young courageous Brave scratching out an existence on the fingernail's edge of the world.

Brave's soul, Shev, was born into the same soul group as Jan-waara. Their soul group had been together for eons. Here in the space in between, souls lived on as eternal flames.

Shevanon and Jan-Waara. Not only were they from the same soul group, but they were also a Soul Pairing. Ages ago, they had chosen each other as soul mates. So, they had chemistry, and they had been born into the Clay many times together. Not always as a loving couple. Sometimes as friends. Sometimes as opponents. Once or twice as family members.

Darius was pondering the best way to contact the Messenger. For the young man, Brave, was attempting a dangerous mission fraught with peril. Not just for himself but possibly for the survival of the latest version of humanity designed for the planet Earth. It was imperative that he find the Island of the Lady. But it was even more important that he connect with the correct female guardian on the island. Together their path forward could be almost magical.

So, Brave could choose to continue his journey with any other guardian from the Island of the Lady. But it would be a lot more guesswork without working with his Soulmate for they knew each other intimately at the cellular level.

If one is familiar with the expression, "It's as if you just read my mind!" Well, that happens most often by weaving together connecting gossamer threads of soul pairings or soul groups. Messages from the Spirit world came through with greater success when soulmates were physically together.

And Brave was going to need all the help he could get to complete this mission while slogging through the Clay. He could connect back to his soul's source with Jan-Waara by his side, for they would create a more powerful transmission.

Yet all along, Shev left a piece of himself behind here in the Spirit world, as a tether of sorts, the trail of breadcrumbs to return home. It is what each soul did when leaving for a 3D expedition on Earth or elsewhere.

When Shev was in Paris, Jan-waara, his soul mate, was embedded in the young child Janette. A long time before that they had struggled as vengeful warriors in the steaming jungles of Southeast Asia torturing their victims in revenge for the loss of their families and village.

But when Shev was born as Sean, the corporate executive, his soul mate, was his wife, Janice. Their love knew no bounds and together they set the world on fire. They had unwound a lot of their past sins throughout that lifetime and taught the world what love could look like by their own passionate relationship.

But hundreds of years later, the world that Sean and Janice knew was long gone. The plays for power and control, the plagues and catastrophes had carried that all away.

Before Shev chose to be born into Brave's body, he made a pact with Jan-waara, his soul's great love. He would find her again, for when they were together, they sparked the physical world around them thus powering the spiritual world. Those souls that chose not to incarnate did not understand the terrible beauty of a free will planet stock full of emotions derived from the sensory experience.

The world was at another pivotal place. It was time for reentry. Souls have extraordinary power, like lightning storms flashing across the sky. When they embed themselves into human vehicles, it feels mucky and difficult. Think about what happens when a lightning bolt hits the Earth, an implosion. When a soul's power works in the physical, it may be a hard slog, but in the space in between, the outcomes are exponential. Literally, stars are born from the sweat of humanity's brow.

Now Shev, as Brave, needed to find Jan-waara again, for optimal support. But these things were delicate, touch and go really. When souls were down in the Clay, there was a lot of what Darius could only term as static interference.

Muttering to himself, Darius grumbled:
"It's as if we are playing a child's game of whisper down the lane. Who knows what distorted message will come out on the other side! Perhaps it is time to employ the expertise of a Dream Weaver at this pivotal point. Hmmm, Charl has developed solid capabilities in this area. But this is critical, we need a master expert for this scenario if we are going to download messages into Brave's dream state."

With long strides Darius continued to pace among the spiraling columns of the Great Library in the sky. He decided it was time to ask Chiara to serve in an advisory capacity for this endeavor. It would not be an easy ask, for much had changed.

In the ever-evolving path of souls, she had relinquished her role as Senior Dream Weaver for deeper duties closer to The Source, from which all creation came forth. She had powered the rebirth of multiple Universes. She had come forth long, long ago, and now the Source was calling her to return. It is akin to a magnetic attraction. Once one starts returning to the terrible, fierce beauty of The Source, it is painful to turn back. For one feels the call in the fabric of the soul. He was asking Chiara to choose painful soul separation for a risky outcome, but he did not see another option.

# INFORMATION BARTER

*40.7831° N, 73.9712° W*

*Island Archipelago, Atlantic Ocean, 2500s*

B rave edged closer to the small clearing in the woods. If the directions provided by the ancient crone were correct, he was now standing on the Island of the Lady. But he had not seen one soul or a hint of anything to prove his presumption.

He thought back over the last leg of his solitary journey. When he had turned South along the coast, he eventually reached a breathtaking sight. He had heard of the great urban centers of their ancestors' past. But to see the grand scale of the remains of one was another thing altogether.

There were all these odd shapes from what must have been their skyscrapers. It was like a giant metallurgist's scrap yard. But now there was moss, lichen, and trees peeping out of every surface. The hard building constructs were slowly devolving back into the soft lines of Mother Earth.

As he wandered through the wonderland, he tried to imagine the number of people that must have once walked the Earth, based on the size of this one place. He shook his head in disbelief.

It was there he had turned one corner and saw a small stream of smoke rising from a fallen building now covered in shrubs and brush. Crouched over the small fire, was an ancient elderly man stoking the flames while his wife was tending a pot.

Their natural expression was one of wariness upon seeing a lone young warrior's approach. Instinctively, he decided to stick with his normal methods of mutual respect. He approached slowly, with his elbows bent, palms spread upward with the latest small game he had shot for his evening meal. As he held out the rabbit in an international sign of reciprocity, their gaze softened into one of hospitality.

How were they surviving here all alone? But Brave was not so sure how alone they really were. He kept his bow near his side and felt for his knives strapped to his thighs, as they settled into a tasty, shared meal.

He knew it was the time to take the risk of human contact, for he needed information to continue his journey in the most efficient manner. One wrong turn could lead to months of misdirection or even death. He needed to find the specific Island of the Lady. There were numerous islands dotting the landscape, it would be nice to know which one he was paddling towards. And of course, he was going to need a boat to do that. Maybe he could barter his hunting skills for a readymade boat.

It was not so easy extracting information since they had no common dialect between them. But he eventually got the question framed with the international language of hand gestures and pictorial dirt drawing with twigs.

"Help me get a boat and identify the Island of the Lady."

It was finally agreed that one deer or a dozen small game equaled his request. But before he went off on the hunt, they agreed to point out the island to him, in a gesture of good faith.

That evening upon his return, a small deer was draped over his shoulders. The elderly couple stood there with watering mouths agape. Quickly it became clear that they had not seen this much meat in an awfully long time.

· • ˙ ‚ ˙ • ˙ ‚ ˙ • ˙ ‚ ˙ • ˙ ‚ ˙ • ˙ ‚ ·

The next morning the aging pair waded into the shallow waters to push his small punt in the rough direction of the Island of the Lady. The old woman looked up into his chocolate brown eyes and said, "Your arrival was foretold in the stars for ages. It is now your time to complete the journey. You must carry the lady's torch forward."

Before he was able to respond, he was past the small tidal break. With a start he stood up in the waffling canoe and shouted back, "Wait!!!" His voice echoed over the waters.

"How do you suddenly know how to speak my dialect? And where is the end of my journey because I do not know where I am going! How will I know when I get there?"

The wizened old pair quickly shrank into the distance, as his small boat leapt into a new current. With despair he wailed in frustration, "And who is this lady?"

# THE FAUN AND THE FLUTE

*40.6895° N, 74.0449° W*
*Island of the Lady, 2500s*

" "The twilight was gloaming," as the bards of old used to pen when there was a plethora of paper still in the world. Brave hovered on the edge of the clearing in the woods on what was purportedly the Island of the Lady.

"Really," Brave began to grumble a bit to himself.

"Who is this mysterious woman after all? I have now walked my solitary path for almost two full moons. The first brought me to the great ocean. This second moon of the year led me along the ocean's southern route of its meandering shore to find this woman. She better be worth it!"

Just as he was about to place his moccasin into the soft mossy grass, he thought he heard the strains of a flute wafting through the forest. But when he strained his ears, he heard nothing. But then it seemed as if it was coming from another direction, more towards his right side.  The sun was setting behind his back, so he could see around the clearing.  The frost was almost crystal dangling from each fern's leaf.

But there it was again!  A soft riff of tinkling notes wafting through the trees.  Then as the mist rose between branches, Brave began to see the movement of a diminutive figure dancing between the trees, with what looked like a flute lifted to a long-shaped face.  Abruptly, he rubbed his eyes, daring the darting figure to clearly appear.

Like a dream, the small creature danced into the clearing, intently playing on a set of pipes that he held to his mouth.  The most ethereal music tinkled from the instrument as if angels were dancing through the small grove.

Was this a dream?  Brave felt an almost magnetic pull towards the small prancing creature.  With surprise, Brave saw that from the torso upwards he was looking at a man.  Yet from the waist down he had the legs and hooves of a deer.  In a flash the dainty thing disappeared into the bracken on the far side of the clearing.

In a trance like state, Brave silently followed the melody of the pipes.  But like a flash, the music died away, and he was once again standing alone.  The wind swept through the branches of the great fir trees whistling its own melody.  Twilight began to settle in liquid pools as Venus rose to play with the stars.

# DOWN THE RABBIT HOLE

*40.6895° N, 74.0449° W*
*Island of the Lady, 2500s*

That night Brave fell quickly into a heavy slumber. Paddling a canoe through unknown currents took a toll on both the mind and the body. He was not long for this world as his body tumbled into much needed sleep. As his mind spun in slower circles, he mumbled to himself, "Yes...tomorrow he would find this mystical lady."

Meanwhile, on the Other Side of things, Darius was prepared. Chiara was so close to The Source now that he did not even have to ask for her help. Silently, her Great Spirit appeared by his side at the opportune time and began to commune with his burdensome thoughts.

Chiara, like no other, could bring the Real into a human's dream-like state. She turned it into a jolting lucid dream that could redirect the rest of that human's life and sometimes alter the course of human history. Somehow, she laced her thoughts through the Dream, making the message more permanently ingrained as part of their destiny. There were many Spirits practicing Dream Weaving skills, but there was only one Chiara.

And it was time to get the message through to the Messenger. Brave turned in his sleep into his dream. He was standing inside of a circular room with whitewashed, stucco walls. They were pearlescent like the inside of a seashell. The luminescence was from dancing flames of fire coming from wall sconces whose soft glow lit the way.

He looked down the spiraling staircase circling away below him. The glittering sconces lit the descent. He felt another man approach on his right. When Brave turned, he saw the bearded lower half of a man's face, whereas the top of his head was covered in what appeared to be a monk's hood. The priest's red beard glistened in the firelight, as his deep voice reverberated, "My name is Februus. Come, for you must perform the cleansing ritual before you venture further. Follow me," as he beckoned Brave to approach the spiraling staircase.

Somehow, they then switched to speaking mind to mind, so he knew that once he reached the bottom of the stairs, all would be revealed. Upon each turn of the stair, Brave dragged the fingers of his right hand along the stucco feeling the drag of the rough surface. It was so physically real to the touch. It could not be a dream anymore.

He was finally going to gain access to the knowledge he needed to complete his calling. He spiraled ever downward in pursuit of answers.

But then he woke to the rays of the rising sun, bathing his face. What was the message? There was something there. If he could just recall what was at the bottom of the stairs. It was painful to grasp for there were no new answers in his mind. He laid there in frustration, his hands clasped in prayer. For the mission was now exacting a toll on both his mind and body.

# METALLURGY

*40.7128° N, 74.0060° W*
*New York City, 2000s*

The cozy King Cole bar was nestled inside the St. Regis Hotel, leaving the blustering February winds howling for attention outside. It was not quite snowing, but it had the feel of it in the air. Sean sat in quiet expectation awaiting Janice's subsequent arrival. He entertained himself by taking the time to admire Maxfield Parrish's dramatic mural filling the wall behind the bustling bartenders.

He could not wait to see Janice's reaction to this nostalgic depiction of Old King Cole, saturated in the romantic colors, reminiscent of the Pre-Raphaelite artists. Secretly, he loved her rebellious rejection of the often soul-lessness found in minimalist art. As a woman proud of her Philadelphian roots, she would hoot with laughter at finding one of her hometown artists so prominently affixed to a wall in an iconic Manhattan bar.

Sean loved the City that Never Sleeps, but Janice not so much. She compared the nearby cities to two brothers. It was as if the City of Brotherly Love was the disrespected little brother, who was tired of standing in his big brother's shadow.

Therefore, after much discussion and a bit of horse trading, Janice finally agreed to meet in New York City for Sean's birthday weekend. Early in the morning, Sean took the Acela train up from Wilmington, Delaware arriving in Penn station. He hosted some customers at The Links Club for lunch. Over time, most of the captains of the chemical and precious metals industries joined this private club. There were many deals that he had discussed in the wood paneled dining room found on the second floor of the traditional brownstone.

They planned to stay in the company's corporate apartment in Midtown, which was a perfect launching point to go visit some of the museums on Janice's list. The apartment's fortieth floor also laid claim to a spectacular view looking down Central Park. Sean looked forward to sharing the panoramas with Janice as he took her in his arms one more time.

It was currently unoccupied, so Sean could reserve it for themselves.

The firm conducted constant business meetings with executives from around the world. It made economic sense to own real estate in this market instead of perpetually paying astronomical hotel prices. This was especially true after Sean negotiated the acquisition price. He had already added some appreciation to this asset of the firm.

He got a text on his Blackberry from Janice that she had found the town car he ordered upon her arrival at LaGuardia. It would not be long now. Besides the museums, Sean had organized one special art experience for them. And as in most things, the best surprises come from the unexpected.

Sir Andrew Featherstone lived in the same high rise where the corporate apartment was located. Through a series of fortuitous events, Sean received an invitation to view the composer's private collection of Pre-Raphaelites that had made it across the pond to his American residency. The romanticized works by this group of inspired artists was right up Janice's alley.

As he waited in a warm haze of expectation to see Janice's glowing face, his mind wandered away to the 1980's to another artistic endeavor, he experienced in New York. He must remember to tell Janice about it.

# GOLD LEAF

*40.7128° N, 74.0060° W*
*New York City, 1980s and the 2000s*

There were only a few times at work where Sean's passion for art directly connected to his world of business. But they were often circumstances contrived by Sean himself, such as the students' art competition that he created for his firm's corporate sponsorship.

Intersections occur in everyone's lives. Some ignore the signals and keep walking straight on by. Others will pause and look down the alternative avenue, but then continue the trodden track. Then there are the few that stop, reflect then veer off onto the path rarely traveled. And it is there that history is often altered.

There was only one time in Sean's hard-working career where Art thrust itself upon his Business life demanding attention. It literally became a symbolic beacon for the world upon his company's success. Upon reflection it still took his breath away.

At the time he was working in North New Jersey. It was back in the 1980's. The company utilized precious metals and applied them to various industrial uses. What they did not use they sold off through their own trading desk on the world's markets.

The company was messily complicated. It was also in dire need of more platinum to make its new-fangled invention, a catalytic converter, work. This new process magically reduced a car's carbon monoxide emissions by the metallurgy of enumerated honeycombed platinum surfaces. Sean was busy practicing international diplomacy in South Africa to gain access to more of the required platinum-group metals, when they got the most unusual of phone calls. It was from the corporate giant of the auto industry, Lee Iacocca.

It all began with President Reagan. He wanted to restore the historic symbol of freedom found in New York's harbor to its original glory, before it splintered into disrepair. The iconic one-hundred and some year-old Statue of Liberty was falling apart at the seams, the metals corroding after a century of exposure to the salty sea air.

In the divisive theater of politics there was little graciousness to approve government funds to restore the beacon to the world. So as is often the case in America, the government's project was turned over to someone who got things done in the private sector. Reagan asked

Iacocca to take the reins of leadership as it would take a personality that could bring many layers together to weave a solution. The CEO was already famous for the resurrection of Chrysler after a solid career in the auto industry. The CEO was now charged with the complex task of restoring the Statue of Liberty to her original glory. But the even more complicated path was funding a budget to pay for it. In this vein, Iacocca began calling on his network of corporate warriors to share his vision and ask for help, in all its varying forms of reciprocation.

There was something about Lady Liberty that pulled at Sean's heart. It was as if she was a part of his personal history already that he had forgotten about. Perhaps he had visited it as a child and couldn't quite recall the trip?

But regardless, he was all in. Internally at Linderwood, Sean was charged with overseeing their firm's contribution to the massive restoration project. It felt like the world was watching because most of it was.

After an exciting discussion, the company board promised to contribute one million dollars of gold bullion that would light the restored torch. After wrestling with some puts and calls to hedge the futures of gold inventory on Linderwood's balance sheet, Sean had a solid plan. Now he felt like the company had a sensible road map of justification for the investor relations team to placate any questioning shareholders.

Interestingly enough, it was again a French artisan that used the painstaking ancient art of gold leaf application to "paint" the torch. The initial modern concept of electroplating was not going to work in the oxidizing salt air. As is often the case, old school methods stand the many tests of time. Every time he came into New York City he looked on the statue's torch with a burst of artistic, patriotic pride.

At that moment, Janice's supple curves were framed in the doorway of the darkened bar backlit by the fluorescent glow of the streetlights behind her. For a moment, her hair was lit like a halo of fire around her silhouetted face. He abruptly stood, and rapidly strode to meet her, despite the disdainful stares of blasé New Yorkers allergic to displays of emotion.

"It's been too long," he whispered into her hair as pictures of Janice wrapped in his arms flashed through his mind. A gay picnic blanket on a hot spring day, lying in the grass at the base of the Statue of Liberty, ignoring strangers' angry stares at their portrait of happiness, looking up to the flashing gold leaf torch lighting the way for humanity.

# EM PATH

*40.6895° N, 74.0449° W*
*Island of the Lady, 2500s*

As Brave wandered out from under the trees, he sensed a presence up ahead before he saw her. But even with his sixth sense pricking, it did not prepare him for what was probably the most spectacular tableau he ever witnessed in his simple life led on the plains. It was clear that THIS was the specific Lady with whom he had been charged to find, and there was nothing that his aging leader could have said that would have prepared him for meeting her face to face, for she was not a human at all. She was the spectacular remains of a fallen metal sculpture, massive in scale.

Her giant form rested supine on her right side, yet all that visibly remained above ground was her massive face fashioned from an antique metalworking process. It must have fallen into its current state of disrepair hundreds of years ago. Today, her only visible aspect was approximately three quarters of her face, which looked freshly excavated based on the newly overturned dirt scattered about. She rested on her right side, and it was as if the void of her left eye was staring into his soul.

From her chin down, where her shoulder must have been, was the beginning of a long earthen mound that stretched back into the trees. The massive mound was covered in lush grasses, shrubs and even a few trees grown into maturity.

The fierce gaze and her terrible size overwhelmed his senses. Drawn like a magnet to the giantess' face, he began to get a sense of her scale. Brave was the tallest man in his tribe, but the width of her cheek bones unfurled above his arm stretched above his head. There were spectacular spires pointing out of her headdress like rays away from the sun.

So taken with the inert sculpture, Brave had not initially sensed another human in the clearing. He could only see the young woman's back as she was busily bent over some work. Her torso was long relative to her legs, even so she was tall for a woman. She was wearing a fur vest like his own, a versatile piece of clothing for the cooler climes where they lived.

Sunlight beamed through the trees turning her back into a burning ember. Most of the vest was made from fox fur, and the umber hues were luxuriant. There seemed to be a few other types of fur stitched into the whole. But the most endearing part of the whole get-up was the switching foxy tail affixed to the hem of the vest. The beautiful red swoosh impeded his view of what must be this woman's most attractive asset.

But it was then this young female turned completely around. His heart stopped in his chest as if he were looking into eternity. Her lips curved into a smile that deserved to be captured in sculptured form too, for future generations. For a moment he forgot where he was, his mission even his name. It was as if he had always known her, and he was finally coming home.

With all the nonchalance in the world, she opened her mouth and quite plainly stated somehow in his own tribe's local dialect:

"Why, hello. You must be the Messenger; we have been waiting for you. Where have you been? Oh, and what do they call you? My name is Em and my tribe is the Path."

Before Brave responded, he thought to himself, "How does everyone else seem to know what I'm supposed to be doing except me? There is something greater afoot here than meets the eye."

He continued to stare as he drank in the whole scene, for if was even more surreal then at first blush. Em was busy at work when he arrived. There was a shovel and a primal pickaxe, that would not get too far based on its condition. There was some fresh dirt removed from around the statue's giant neck, it appeared this was an ongoing archaeological dig.

She raised the back of one hand to swipe at a few streaks of dirt.

A few feet away there were some modest supplies where she was mixing a concoction to remove the green patina from the massive copper face. However, the work was difficult. So far there were only a few spots that had returned to the original copper color after all of her laborious effort.

Brave thought to himself, "She could spend the rest of her life out here trying to unearth a giant and remove generations of corrosion."

But the most amazing thing he saw in his assessment of the clearing, if you could discount everything already described, was spread out in front of Em, on a giant rock. It was the beginning of a drawing of the sculpture. But it was not the drawing itself that shocked Brave, it was the surface that Em was using for it was something close to the lost ancient process of paper making! Brave had never seen paper anywhere except those few ancient crumbling books that were his tribe's most treasured relics.

Before he responded formally to Em's introduction, in a few long bounds he was by her side and knelt before her drawing. In his young rudimentary life, he was drawn to chemical and mechanical processes. He thirsted for knowledge and always wanted to learn how to make things. Quietly, he mourned the lost magic of their ancestors' technological accomplishments.

Breathlessly Brave asked, "How did you make paper?"

It was not like the ancients' fine paper delicately bound into books. It was more of a spongy board made of wood pulp and resins, probably heated, and cooled. It seemed that she had also taken charcoal from a hearth and compressed it somehow into a crumbling but solid tool that she could draw and shade with.

With a touch of startled amusement, the corner of Em's lip curled up along with one eyebrow. So much had gone through Brave's mind in this moment, he realized he had never answered Em's question. Stumbling into protocol,

"My name is Brave, and yes I am the Messenger. But I have no idea what that means. But the one thing I DO now know, is that I have completed the first leg of my journey. And that was to find the Lady of this Island and to find you. For here you both are."

With that Brave turned and gave a small nod of respect to the huge sculpture slowly being resurrected by Em's careful excavation. Then his eyes turned back to meet hers again. They were deep dark pools the color of the rich earth. He saw flickers of recognition somewhere in their depths as he continued to speak to this stranger as if she was his kin.

"You are the agent I was charged to find, and it is your knowledge that must lead us on from here. For it is clear you know much more of the lost civilization that lived here before us. It was foretold that now is the time that we can access their lost knowledge."

With a singular stare, Em tested, "How do you know that I am the one?"

Brave felt the sharp edges of her mind, with a quiver of excitement he recognized the same joy he received when physically sparring with his sporting competitors. But this was much more pleasurable, for he had found a mental match who could push him to pursue deeper knowledge. And right now, he was at a disadvantage, for his mind was completely overtaken by her human skin. With a quick shake of his shaggy locks, he tried to shake out the cobwebs, so he could properly respond.

"Well for one, I have no idea how you know the words of my tribe. I have come far, I walked for two full moon circuits to find you. When we trade with tribes nearby, we use a lot of hand gestures, for we cannot understand each other very well. We have all lived apart for so long to minimize the spread of plagues. But here you are speaking to me in words I can understand."

With a cool appraising stare she responded, "You wouldn't believe me if told you. But yes, I am the one, and I have been waiting for you for a long time. I've been preparing for your arrival and our next course of action."

"Tell me about the Lady. Who was she?" Brave could not contain his curiosity any longer.

A small mist unfurled its tendrils wrapping itself around the prone statue and crept towards their ankles. Em's inscrutable gaze turned tender as she looked lovingly on her sculptured ward.

She half-whispered in a reverential tone, "She was an especially important symbol to the great civilization that lived here long ago before they were snuffed out. In fact, she became a beacon to that ancient world."

With that solemn remembrance they both paused and performed the mudra for divine worship. They pressed both palms together, fingers straight all touching in that international sign of prayer and supplication. After the near extinction of humanity, and subsequent great diaspora, hand gestures seemed to be the only remaining commonality between the scattered tribal groups.

When they came together for barter and trade, hand signals were the pragmatic useful tool. But specifically, the praying hands gesture was the international sign for gratefulness. For they were all descendants of the remnant that survived. Anytime their ancestors' memory was invoked, it was a common way to express their thanks.

"What do you mean a beacon for the world?" Brave asked.

He sat down on the edge of the boulder where Em was working, placing his chin in his palm, expectantly waiting for more of the story. She walked towards the huge face and touched the lips as she began her narrative.

"As we know much of the written records have been lost. Like your tribe, we have a few sacred books from our ancestors that we protect. But much passed down in our tribe's oral legends and a few other methods."

Her preemptive knowledge about his tribe and her cryptic comment about other methods did not escape Brave. He had grown into an impeccable listener. But he did not want to interrupt the story's flow, he would find out about this later.

Em continued, "But this is what we do now know about the Lady of our Island. The Ancients called her The Statue of Liberty. We saw some records of Libertas, but we think that was an older language from before. They called this land A-mare-ick-uh. I know it sounds strange, and it does not have anything to do with a horse. It was named after an explorer that came from across the great sea." Em paused pointing East towards the ocean.

"After these explorers came across, they brought settlers to live in this resource rich land. They called this The Great Experiment, because it was the first time in human history where a government tried to give its people personal liberty. At some point, people from the other side of the ocean saw how much the new A-mare-ikuh was growing and believed it was because of this recognition of freedom. There were two men in a country called Frah-nz that collaborated to make and then give Lady Liberty as a gift. An artist named Barth-oldy possibly and a patron. There was an engineer named Eye-Full that designed the metal skeleton to support her massive form. She was very costly and complicated to make and send here. It got the world's attention long ago."

With that Em started using hand gestures mimicking a person reading from papers in hand. In frustrating futility, she said, "It was when paper was as common as grass and everyone could read something if they chose. They had tools that sent knowledge everywhere…they would put the story about our Lady Liberty on papers around the world…"

It seemed like Em's lower lip was trembling from holding back tears of sadness over the disappearance of so much knowledge and common communication.

Politely, Brave turned towards Lady Liberty and began to examine her ancient patina. Up close there was a lot of crackling. Being under the earthen mound for so long must have helped protect her from the elements of air and sea some. He was quite touched by what was apparently Em's solo attempt to unearth and restore the massive Lady.

After Em collected herself a bit, she appeared by his side to resume her story:

"But Lady Liberty isn't the only giant mystery to be unraveled here. There was another even more ancient race that lived across the land before the A-mare-ick-uns. We now know of them as the Mound Builders."

With that Em's eyes turned towards the forest where the mist was even thicker. It was as if she was weighing how much she was willing to share at this early stage of their acquaintance. Brave stood quietly, barely breathing so he would not disturb her self-imposed trance. He had never heard of this race, he wanted to know more. But she seemed to need a bit of prodding, so he murmured, "The Mound Builders."

With a gentle start, her eyes refocused on the present and she whispered, "Yes the Mound Builders. They were human, but they were different from us. They lived all over this great land."

With a quick spin on her heel, Em strode towards the darkening wood. "Come I will show you."

# SHAPESHIFTER

*40.6895° N, 74.0449° W*
*Island of the Lady, 2500s*

As Sean entered the forest, he kept his eyes on Em's back, for she was a shapeshifter just like the fox whose fur she wore. Silently, she twisted through the trees.

Suddenly, he felt a charge of energy flood through him as he recognized the scene. He recalled another forest, time, and place, where he and this mystical woman were stalking prey together in the forest, he could still smell the pungent loam of the earth as he knelt to check for tracks. They wore similar fur vests, but then they were both men. And Em was then his bodyguard. That old version of Em would circle around to his back, walking backwards with an arrow ready to spring from a drawn bow.

Even though it was only a daydream, it gave Sean a sense of security to trust Em at a deeper level, even with his life. For it seemed that he had already trusted her with this many other times.

# SIDEBAR

*Space in Between Time*

D arius stood stock still in the Tapestry Room looking down at two vibrating strands. The two strands represented Sean and Em, and before his eyes the two distant threads snapped together and wrapped around each other.

To some of the weavers in the room it appeared that Darius had a tear in his eye. He exhaled deeply and turned to the Great Master, Chiara, swirling peacefully at his side. For the first time in a while, Darius' lips formed a small smile.

Gravely he bowed his head in thanks to Chiara as he spoke:

"We all can't thank you enough for your master dream weaving skills. Your promptings of humans while they are in their REM or daydream states is quite magical to observe. To remind Sean of their previous life together in another primitive past as they entered the wood was pure art. As time is of the essence, getting

Sean and Em connected quickly and reminding them of their already existing rapport of trust was imperative. If humanity's survival were not hanging on their mission, I would be much more joyful than I appear. Right now, I just feel utter relief."

Chiara's soul was closing in on her return journey to The Source from whence all souls splintered off during their birth. Her soul force was now so powerful that she did not use words too much anymore even here in the space between. Instead, she downloaded information into other Souls, mind to mind.

Chiara's spirit began to transmit love into Darius' soul, he was overwhelmed by its depth and purity. Through this process, Darius began to realize how deeply Chiara loved humanity and their resident planet, despite their self-destructive efforts. Through this transmission, he came to realize that Chiara was one of the significant guardians of Mother Earth. She was in the process of transitioning this responsibility to another spirit as she completed her return to The Source. It became clearer to him that Earth was indeed a linchpin in The Source's grand design of the multi-Universes it had created and powered.

There were many other worlds across the spectrum, but Earth was tucked off in an isolated corner, where conducting risky experiments would not be as dangerous to other life forms. The thing that was special about Earth was it was one of the very few places granted autonomous free will. So yes, they were most definitely the rebellious child in the universal family. But when even one of them freely chose selfless love, it unleashed an unbelievable wave of creative power that rolled through space and time.

It was something about their autonomous choice of love that literally made not only worlds spin round but whole Universes. However, their acts of hatred could also destroy other innocents. Now Darius fully understood that Chiara was giving her wayward children one more motherly act of guidance before she passed this torch to another guardian. The terrible beauty of it all brought real tears from Darius' spirit in a display of human emotion.

They dropped onto the tapestry as Chiara's form burned a fire engine red embracing him one more time, before she dissipated into a fine mist. With great heaving sobs, Darius knew it was the last time he would interact with Chiara as an individual soul. She gave him this last parting gift. He knew the next part of the race was now his burden to carry. But there was a small flame of love burning deep in his soul that Chiara lit in that last enveloping embrace. He knew he was not alone really. Chiara was just a few steps ahead of him, as all souls eventually returned from their tireless travels and reunited with The Divine Source of them all.

# THE SURPRISING
# TWO ANDREWS

*40.7128° N, 74.0060° W*
*New York City, 2000s*

J anice and Sean took the elevator up to the 56th floor of the skyscraper. Janice still had no idea of what was in store for her. It had been difficult to keep the surprise to himself, but he managed to do it.

The tinkling of crystal glasses and the murmur of subdued conversation leaked through the dark mahogany door. She turned to give Sean a questioning look, as she wove her left hand through the crook of his arm. It was not always a natural gesture for them as a couple, for Janice was a tall woman, making them equal in stature when barefoot. Now, Janice in heels was a sight to behold; the goddess Athena came to mind.

With that the door opened, and Janice's jaw dropped in shock. For, their host for the evening was the famous Sir Andrew Featherstone. Sean broke into a smile, for he had finally surprised his wife.

Yes, their host was a knighted gentleman, and a world-renowned composer. But he also held possibly the largest private collection of Pre-Raphaelite art, which was the highlight of this evening's salon.

As the night unfolded, Sean's heart burst with pride, as he watched Janice learn about this amazing selection directly from its collector. Like many artistic movements, the Pre-Raphaelites were a rebellion against the restraints of the popular art regime of their time. Dante Gabriel Rossetti and a few other artists were incensed that Raphael of the Italian Renaissance had just been inducted into the Royal Academy. They wanted to harken back to the good old Medieval days when there were knights of yore and everything was quote, simple and natural. They disliked the ornate contrivances of the highly stylized Renaissance art represented by Raphael.

As Janice's private tour came to an end, she returned to Sean's side still dazed from the colorful visual spectacle and intellectual stimulation.

Still mystified, Janice asked, "But how do you two know each other? I know you both have places here in the same apartment building, but so do thousands of other people."

Sean, a great storyteller, began, "Well it all started one day, when the Executive Director of the Delaware Art Museum, Steve, received a call. The inquirer asked about the museum's collection of Pre-Raphaelite art. It was our host, Mr. Featherstone! Immediately upon hanging up, Steve called me next as I was the current Chairman of the Board."

Sean's voice began to vibrate as he warmed to the story, "Our host had an amazing request, after reading a recent article about our museum's collection. Until that point, he had been sure that he had the largest collection of this genre. Now he was not so sure, so he wanted to come and see for himself!"

By that point, the miscellaneous conversations common to a cocktail party murmured to a halt, as Sean's vibrating baritone often could mesmerize its listeners. The subject of Sean's story was enjoying the moment as well, as he sank down into a high-backed wing chair, crossed one knee over the other, waving one elegant hand to continue.

With that signal of approval, Sean continued in those luxuriant velvety tones that made Janice's ears ring: "Well, I wasn't going to miss that adventure for anything in the world! Now, I am not sure who's idea this was, probably Steve's, as he was creative like that. But somehow we cooked up the idea to make this a really special day for our host to remember our little museum."

After a small dramatic pause, Sean continued, "So, Steve called up our most famous local artist, Andrew Wyeth, of the "*Helga* Pictures and *Christina's World*" fame.

We asked if he would be interested in serving as our docent for the planned private tour and he said yes!"

You could hear the sharp intake of breath across the room of Manhattanites, since Andrew Wyeth was not a favorite of New York's art critic world, as he refused to conform to their stipulations. Janice raised a hand to disguise the smirk on her lips.

Sean barreled on, "When Sir Featherstone, arrived at our Museum, he was impeccably dressed. Not to be outdone, Mr. Wyeth evoked his own flare for the dramatic. Mr. Wyeth had on a white suit, white shoes, white socks, a white shirt." You could hear a titter go across the crowd of New Yorkers, most of which dressed in their own uniform of cosmopolitan black.

With a smile Sean was not finished, "A white hat, a white cane, and a white cape that was lined in flaming red!"

You could hear murmurs of things like, only an artist. Sean continued his recount of events:

"It was an amazing afternoon, to have the honor of being the proverbial fly on the wall, and listen to these two great men talk about art. They were analyzing brush strokes, trading stories and bits of knowledge with each other."

One of the guests asked of Featherstone, "So who had the greater collection?"

Ever gracious their host replied, "It was the chair designed by William Morris that they procured. It was painted by Rossetti himself, *"The Arming of a Knight."* That one piece brought me to concede to the Delaware Art Museum. It was unique!"

After a pause Featherstone quipped, "However, I still believe, I have the largest PRIVATE collection!" This last remark was received with much laughter.

The evening wore on. As everyone was leaving and saying their good-byes, Janice paused by one small painting near the apartment's front door. It was titled *Februus* on the small frame's plaque.

Janice murmured out loud, "I recall learning that the month of February is named after Februus, a Greek god, or is it Roman?"

However, despite the mythological title, the work was in the brushy deconstructed strokes of the French Impressionists. It made use of a lot of gay but natural colors of the forest. All of which made it that much more intriguing, for the painting depicted a half human form, consisting of a man's torso and head, but with the legs of a faun. It was as if Janice had seen it somewhere before. But where? And who was the artist? She leaned towards the painting, squinting a bit since her reading glasses were tucked in her purse, was it J. Laurent? Or was that an I?

Before she could satisfy her curiosity by interrogating their host, she was bundled into her coat by her husband's burly, loving hands. As he wrapped his powerful arm around her waist, he leaned over and whispered into her ear, "I know that investigatory look of yours. *Februus* will have to wait, for right now, I need you all to myself. It has been too long."

# INTO THE FOREST

*40.6895° N, 74.0449° W*
*Island of the Lady 2500s*

E m led the reluctant Brave into the dense trees. It was difficult to walk away from the beautiful Lady Liberty. For he had never seen such a large man made metal object before. Throughout his conversation with Em, he kept returning to stare into the statue's vacant eyes. He estimated that her one eye was a little less than the length of his long arm.

It felt like a portal into the past. By gazing on her ancient remains, he was beginning to form his own sense of the massive scale of their ancestors' sophistication. Sadness filled him as he pondered their near extinction and their dazzling enlightenment. A-mare-ikuh had once been a beacon of light for a world that no longer existed anywhere.

Before they turned into the trees, Brave knelt in silent genuflection before the statue, honoring their predecessors' lost advances and greatness. Some sense of survivor's guilt, more like responsibility, draped itself around his shoulders like a cloak. He felt even more determined to complete all that he could of his mysterious mission. For if he could help unravel the mysteries of these ancient peoples, maybe they could regain some of the technological miracles for today! They could all rest a bit easier rather than scrabbling along a knife's edge for basic survival.

As he walked away, he felt her majestic metallic stare boring holes into his back. He could not help but murmur, "I will try my best."

He turned to Em and again fell under the spell of her fathomless, warm brown eyes. He said solemnly, "I will follow you." In his head he completed the sentence with "anywhere, anytime, anyplace and for always."

# THE MOUND BUILDERS

*40.6895° N, 74.0449° W*
*Island of the Lady 2500s*

As they stepped carefully through the forest, Em began to tell stories about what they were about to see. There was evidence of another more ancient race before their ancestors, the A-mare-ikuns. It was deep underground, and one of their tribal leaders cared for the space. Their Tribe of the Path deemed it as sacred and believed that it was one of the keys to unlocking their lost ancient human heritage.

Em began to speak in her preferred matter of fact tone, which was quite ironic really. Every time she opened her mouth, she shattered his world view. For she had already told him more about their ancestors' lost civilization than he had ever known before. And now she was telling him about an even more ancient race before the A-mare-ikuns that he had never heard referenced in his own village.

"First, we called them The Old, Old Ones. But as we learned more about them, we discovered they created these massive earthen works all over our continent. So, we named them The Mound Builders."

"How do you know they are a different race from a different time? It was all so long ago," Brave asked.

They were walking single file through the trees, with Em leading. She paused, turned around and looked directly into his eyes. Without blinking she responded, "They were giants."

Shock sent a chill down Brave's body and wrapped his tongue in speechlessness. With that she picked up a tree branch. She gently tapped his shoulder.

"Their long legs ended about right here. And they were about this tall."

With that she tapped the branch's tip against a nearby tree trunk, about four feet above Brave's head.

"But you will see for yourself. Oh, and we found The Old, Old Ones' bones with totally different animal bones. They were giants too. Our ancestors named them dyno-sars."

They came to a slab of rocky ridge cresting from the ground. Em walked up to its face and crouched down. She turned into what had been an invisible crevice then disappeared from his view. He stepped forward turning to see the small opening. He could just make out the swish of her vest's foxy tail in the dim light. His broader frame was a tighter squeeze through the narrow opening, but he got through and dropped down onto the dry, scrabbly floor of the cave.

After their eyes adjusted to the dim light, they moved forward single file through a long natural hall for about fifty feet until it veered sharply left. Once they made the turn, Brave could see bright torch light blazing through a narrow crack a bit further ahead.

Em reached out her hand and pulled back what appeared to be a flap of animal skins hanging like a door to a tent. After approaching in near darkness, the brightness was blinding. It was as if they stepped inside the interior of a chambered nautilus seashell.

The room was circular in shape. It was a natural rock formation; however, the walls had a stucco applied by human hands. Brave was spellbound for he had been in this very room before. However, it was in his dream. There was the same circular staircase spiraling down into the earth, a miraculous engineering feat for sure. The only stairs he had ever seen before was the rough steps hewn into the riverbank. This was another matter altogether.

He approached the stairwell to peer down into the light glowing from below. Just as in the dream, the same red bearded man in a monk-like robe stepped forward from the shadows and said, "Welcome. My name is Februus."

At this point, nothing could surprise Brave anymore. His tribe taught to always pay attention to dreams as they could carry messages. Often, they were confusing, but an Elder could often decipher the hidden meaning. In this case the prophetic vision of his current surroundings gave Brave the comfort he needed to trust the situation and the two people he was with. He had no idea how it had happened, but it did affirm that he must be on the right track.

Just as in his dream, Brave followed the man down the spiraling staircase, but in this case, Em was there right behind him. When they reached the bottom, Em walked over to the wall and grasped one of the wall torches in her hand. She beckoned Brave to take one for himself. He followed her down another darkened hall to an empty room. She knelt, as the flames' light flickered across the smooth floor.

With a gasp, Brave saw yet another amazing sight. Lady Liberty was already the biggest surprise in his young life, now he was experiencing the second in one day!

There were fossilized skeletal human remains set in stone. But it was a giant of a human. Brave knelt in astonishment by Em's side. Like two children making snow angels, the pair laid down on their backs next to it. Their own heads ended somewhere just above the navel of this very human skeleton. He or she appeared to have been surprised by death, then captured in this final moment. The skull was huge, it could have fit over Brave's own head as a hat. The teeth were perfectly formed. Upon a closer look, there were two rows of them!

By now Februus entered the space and held his torch aloft so Brave could take in more of the room. With another gasp he drank in another riveting sight: his first view of a massive animal's skeletal remains. This must be what Em called a dyno-sar. It made the giant human look small. If he had not seen it for himself, he would not have been able to comprehend the scale of either of these creatures.

His finger crept over and stroked the bones of the human's fingers. Like a shock of electricity, he felt connected in some way to this massive figure.

Februus spoke, "These bones hold many answers to our questions. They explain where we came from and who was here before us. We now must work together to unlock their secrets. For they were a mighty race. Mightier than our own ancestors, the A-mare-ikuns. It is taught that at one time in our ancient planet's past, the Old, Old Ones lived all around the world. They taught us the secrets of agriculture to further our human survival. But then something happened that wiped them out. Maybe they knew the world's changing climate would no longer support their giant race?"

With a quiet pause, Februus closed his eyes as if in remembrance, then continued, "We think that is why they created us. Perhaps our smallness was more suited to changes in air and gravity? We do not really know, but we do know this. It is important for humans to survive here on Earth, for we have a calling. A universal mission we must complete. Right now, we are at a pivotal point. If we can access the lost secrets of our ancestors, the A-mare-ikuns and the Mound Builders before them, we can progress with some technical advances."

Februus bowed his hooded head. Then with a dramatic flair, he pushed it back from his large skull, so one could see each red hair glisten in the flames. His blue eyes flashing with intensity. He finished his statement with, "Otherwise, we may go extinct too. Our Universe needs us to do our part and that is to live, as our expended energy powers Universes in some mysterious way."

# UNLOCKING FEBRUUS

*48.8566° N, 2.3522° E*
*Paris, France 1870's*

T he Laurent family was arranged around their dining table again, the detritus of a sumptuous meal was being cleared by the countryside maids. It was not an easy time in France, as the Franco-Prussian War had just ended, and the beginning of its Third Republic was in its infancy.

In these trying times, finding good help in Paris was nigh on impossible. Through their neighborhood's butcher shop, Madame Laurent was able to hire one farming family's five daughters. They somehow had survived the war but needed work any which way they could find. They were from a sturdy stock, but still had much to learn of the required social refinements of Parisian table service for the cosmopolitan class.

Madame Laurent was at her zenith when entertaining guests at their beautifully appointed home.

She had a knack for bringing together interesting people from varying professions and walks of life. It created an atmosphere for engaging conversations and the exchange of exciting new ideas.

But this particular evening, Madame had entered a new stratosphere. The evening was electric, for she had secured the attendance of Messieurs Eiffel, Bartholdi and de Laboulaye. They were in the middle of an amazing collaboration of their own, the design and construction of Lady Liberty.

Bartholdi had just returned from America where he was successful in receiving more private donations to further fund the beautiful statue. Monsieur was in the middle of describing the moment he saw the island in New York's harbor that was the perfect spot for the massive installation. The guests listened in awestruck wonder.

The scintillating conversation continued, as Eiffel described the moment, he grasped the required internal architectural framework. His mathematics had to be quite precise to support the massive copper sheets that Bartholdi was hammering into the Lady's external shape.

It also became clear that de Laboulaye's role as spokesperson was imperative as well. He was the global project's natural fundraiser. It was a daunting undertaking, which required significant funding and promotion. But he was born with the silver tongue, and somehow, he inspired donors to pitch in often before he ever had to ask.

The daring vision manifesting into the physical was awe-inspiring. Throughout the course of the evening, it became clear that the massive Lady Liberty would have remained a figment of imagination, if the trio had refused to work with each other.

As Bartholdi told his part of the adventurous tale, he spoke of the pulsing energy he found so invigorating when he visited America. As a point of emphasis, he pulled out of his left breast pocket a neatly folded newspaper article that he extracted from an American paper during his travels.

With his long, tapered fingers, he smoothed the article out on the tablecloth as he began to speak:

"These Americans have a solid work ethic laced with curiosity and adventure. For example, they are obsessed with land as they are a heavily agrarian society. As they expand, the farmers are tilling new soil all the time. In their toils, across the entire nation, they have uncovered the most amazing remains and artifacts of a distant ancient race. Apparently, these discoveries are so prevalent they are reported daily in papers across the great nation. But that is not the most astonishing fact. Here listen for yourselves, here is an example, in the New York Tribune."

The sculptor paused, delicately smoothed the creases out from the displayed article and began to read to the party:

"Ancient human remains have been found at Mount Morris. But the skeleton is of a giant. Besides its extreme stature, the ancient human had two rows of still perfect teeth. Along with the enormous bones are man made articles fashioned from metals. The newly formed Smithsonian Institute plans to secure the skeleton and artifacts for further research."

"I know it sounds shocking to us. But the American farmers are so used to it now, they find it almost common. The ancient discoveries always seem to be in these massive earthen mounds, where this race must have buried their dead. The Americans know these mounds must be ancient, because beside grass growing over them, there often are huge oak trees growing out of the mounds themselves! And we know how a tree's ring represents one year in the life of a tree!"

The room had grown quite still, silent in fact as they contemplated this astonishing monologue about the New World. The dinner guests began to pass the newspaper story from hand to hand so they could read it for themselves.

Bartholdi finished with a flare, "So the New World perhaps isn't so new after all! Perhaps America was the Old World, and we are just rediscovering it?"

A bit more dreamily, a young man at the table finished the strange new concept with,

"Perhaps it is as the Biblical Pentateuch says, "it was when giants still walked the Earth."

Mademoiselle Janette was raptly listening to this thought-provoking conversation, as a young French lady should in the presence of her elders. However, for Janette social settings beloved by her mother were often painful for the young lady. Even though she was born into a prominent Parisian family, she never felt like she quite belonged in her Mother's sparkling Salons. She longed to tiptoe up the stairs to her secret artist studio to sit amongst the rafters and paint. However, throughout these tedious evenings she felt her Mother's watchful eye cataloguing each of her movements. She felt just like their pet canary in the gilded cage: trapped and on display for perennial inspection.

But this evening was a bit different. Janette was not a sculptor, but she still found the thrill of the adventurous story titillating as she imagined the scale of the Lady Liberty. But on a more personal level, Janette was thrilled to also see Monsieur Durand Ruel in attendance. He had just returned from London, where he recently moved his art business, to further insulate it from the perpetual continental wars.

Monsieur was now a personal hero of Janette's after all he was the first person to express belief in her paintings. The last time she saw his bearded face was the night her life was given further purpose. For the art procurer had kindly taken three of her paintings away with him for exhibition and sale.

Of course, as a young lady from a distinguished family they were required to be exhibited under a pseudonym to protect her reputation. On the spur of the moment the generous businessman suggested that they list the paintings for sale under her surname, Laurent, as if they were her father's works. Since she had already signed them J. Laurent, there was no need for any changes, as she and her father shared the same initial on their first names: J.

As the sparkling evening's sizzling fire fizzled to an ember-ed glow, Durand-Ruel moved to stand to make a final toast. With the well-timed pause of one accustomed to commanding a room through force of personality, he began with a brief bow to their hostess:

"I must thank you for a lovely evening at one of the most interesting dinner tables in Paris. I can only repay your hospitality in kind through my service. Your family has given me the privilege of representing you, even if somewhat clandestinely, with a number of artistic works that were made within these walls."

With this pronouncement, Janette's seated posture improved to the ninety degree angle her Mother wished she could always retain. Her skin pricked all over as her artistic endeavors moved to the forefront of the conversation.

"I now have the great pleasure of informing Monsieur Laurent that his household has sold one of these Avant Garde paintings, for a modest sum. I am pleased to present a check for the net proceeds, after expenses of course. I've also taken the liberty of creating a bill of sale in Monsieur's name as the named artist."

With a brief bow to his host, Durand Ruel finished with, "The patron selected *Februus*, primarily because of the emotion captured in the paint swirls, very modern. The colors remind one of the natural hues of the forest and nature. The painting's title was quite an engaging point of dialogue with the buyer. For it showcases the ably equipped mind of the artist, to place the ancient Etruscan and Roman god for ritual purification into a modern work of this sort. It is a sophisticated effort. Only someone with subtlety who was also taught ancient concepts could enmesh the two so cleanly."

Monsieur Laurent completed a failed half-attempt at suppressing a grin, a facial expression that often found its way to his otherwise serious face when the subject matter was his daughter.

He replied, "Well, I must say I am pleased to serve as my daughter's ghost artist, as I have no ability nor care to lift a finger to canvas. Also, Janette's tutors have taught her well. As Februus, oft represented in the form of a faun, is also found to be the God of prosperity. Therefore, her subject matter has been fruitful," he finished with a small dash of humor.

By this point all motion around the table had ceased. Janette had launched from her chair in a most unladylike manner, placing both hands over her mouth in shock as tears started flowing down both cheeks. As she glanced towards her Mother, she was startled to find her Mother speechless with her own mouth gaping.

With a strangled gasp, Janette cried, "Oh! Someone likes my work! And I am so glad they took *Februus*. He needs to be looked after..."

With that Janette skipped around the table to the art dealer's seat and wrapped her arms around his broad shoulders in an unexpected embrace. She bent down and whispered in his ear,

"Thank you for believing in me. I will never be able to explain how much this means to me!"

With that Janette skipped towards the doorway ready to race up the stairs to her paints in the attic before realizing she had forgotten all her manners. She turned to face her mother, her hands clasped in prayer,

"Oh Mother, will you please excuse me at this time? For I have a matter to which I must attend."

For once her Mother was speechless. Amazed that what she viewed as her daughter's folly was valued by others. But as most relationships between mothers and daughters are complex in their many layers, so was this one. For the first time, Janette saw secret maternal pride filling up the whites of her mother's eyes. And it was suddenly enough between them. Maybe her Mother did not fully appreciate or understand her passionate drive to create this new art form. But she was now proud that her daughter's achievement was recognized by those who mattered in her social set.

After receiving that motherly nod of dismissal, Janette bounded up the stairs towards her future, embracing her persona as the artist, J. Laurent. Grateful for the permission to finally embrace her destiny. For Janette, the fact that her fate was also cloaked in anonymity suited her well. Invisibility had long been her favorite wardrobe choice. Therefore, it was now a comfortable disguise.

# TAPESTRY VISIT

*The Space in Between Time*

D arius, the great spirit master paced the floor between the tapestry weavers. The weavers were the thread-minders, which were quite alive forging their own paths. The weavers were the shepherds watching the flock to ensure that no sheep wandered over a cliff or strayed too far. As he turned towards the door, the merry trio of Jan-Waara, Shevanon and Charl, appeared which brought a ghost of a smile to Darius' lips. The three souls were enjoying this brief hiatus in each other's company. A respite from all their serious endeavors.

Darius remembered when their soul group was created, what an electric bunch. Their little misadventure in the great Spirit Library came to mind. What an energetic group. He would never forget the day when the mortified librarian rushed in to complain about their mischievous activities. This crew had decided to reenact one of the historical sea battles they were studying by rearranging all the stacks of books into armadas of ships, as they nimbly ran up and down the stacks thrusting and parrying imaginary swords. All the baby souls were sitting on the floor laughing and pointing at the irreverent use of dusty volumes. Darius recalled laughing at Charl's explanation that "they were trying to make boring history come alive."

This is when Jan-Waara earned her nickname of Jan, as her teachers got tired of correcting her classroom shenanigans such as energy discharges and other pranks. And probably that is where Shevanon's nickname Shove began. Darius shook his head again as he recalled Shove shoving books over the edge of the library desks pretending that they were cannon balls.

Of the three, Charl, rarely incarnated on Earth anymore. He had finished all his necessary 3D prerequisites on Earth. He had spent several lifetimes as Jan's protector, so he held a greater Earthly dimensional connection with her than he did with Shev.

Therefore, as a dream weaver he could more easily send her important messages to her in dreams. Even though he and Shev were also in the same soul group, Charl was not as accurate getting downloads into Shev's dreams when he was in human body.

Logically, the obstacle made sense, in that any connection souls have with each other in the space in between does not translate so well into the 3D reality of an Earthly life. There is a lot of static or interference due to the heaviness of the material.

Therefore, they worked well as a Triumvirate, which they were now doing across multiple timelines. Normally, Charl remained on the Spirit side of things to formulate and deliver the instructional downloads for Shove and Jan to execute while operating on Earth. Based on Charl's extensive time spent in 3D lives with Jan his signal connectivity was better with her. The important reminders transmitted more accurately and completely into Jan's dreams and thoughts.

Down in the miry clay, upon waking or returning from a meditative state, Jan communicated on many levels with Shev via their intense body-mind-soul connection. From their many incarnated lives together, there was a deep implicit trust between them.

Then Shev's many, many lives as a fearless warrior fighting for freedom, truth and justice made Shev the optimal executioner of difficult sometimes impossible tasks. He could shove more accomplishments into one lifetime then many souls. He did not always choose well, but he sure did know how to choose and get something done.

This was the lesson that Shev was still working on while in an incarnation. How to listen and connect better with that Divine sill voice within so he would execute the optimal choice. He had too often taken justice into his own hands and that was still rippling through eternity. How does one choose more wisely when wading through the muck?

This is where the trio was banding together more tightly. Jan-Waara and Charl were practicing their transmission skills. At the same time, she and Shev were tuning up their soul connectivity in the healing springs, especially for their lives as Brave and Em. They needed to be completely on the same page.

Darius brought them together around a perfectly round stone table in a windowed alcove just off the Tapestry Room. They outlined all the messages they planned to deliver to Jan in her multiple Earthly lifetimes. For they were all interconnected with each other and they affected future outcomes for the remains of humanity. There were three messages to transmit to Jan while she was experiencing three key Earthly incarnations. One to Janette, the bonne femme garret-artiste. The second one was for Janice living the modern urban love story with her beloved Sean, the charging executive. Then three, perhaps the most pivotal messages were to Em. For she was now the main transmitter of higher knowledge and direction to Brave, as his tribe lost one of the Twelve Elders before he was born.

Darius bowed his head as he contemplated the massive swath of humanity lost during the wars and plagues. It was coming down to the end game there were only so many moves remaining. If they did not get this right during Brave and Em's incarnation, the threads could possibly unravel, and another root race might be entirely lost again.

The four of them bowed their heads and asked for the Divine's help as they formed their intricate plans.

# A DIVINE MESSENGER

*40.6895° N, 74.0449° W*
*The caves on the Island of the Lady*

Em and Brave looked at Februus' fair features in the dancing flames. Em had seen the priest on occasion as part of the village's fabric of life. But his hooded cowl mostly hid his eyes from view. Now she understood why. It protected him from the sun's radiating rays and their brown-eyed startled stares. For he did not look like them at all.

Not many humans had blue eyes anymore. The survivors that made up the remnant were mostly of darker complexion with fathomless dark eyes. Most people only half-believed that there used to be multitudes with hair the colors of the setting sun and eyes the color of the sky. Apparently, their genetic markers were not as resistant to the variety of killer plagues. By the time the world's population whittled down to the decimated remnant of humanity, there were very few of the lightly complected alive.

But here was this priest of the underground as documentation of this near extinct ethnic diversity. As if reading their minds, Februus replied to their thoughts,

"Yes, I am one of the few carrying the recessive traits. It is difficult for me to live above ground full time, for my eyes and skin are now too sensitive to our current atmospheric conditions. I can come outside around sunset and in the evenings. Your tribes' darker complexions have adapted quite nicely over the last several hundred years to today's harsher environment."

His blue irises were quite mesmerizing. It was disconcerting as one could almost see into his emotions and thoughts. It was like watching clouds scudding across a robin's egg blue sky. He continued simply:

"I am one of the Twelve."

There was silence. Em felt like she intuitively knew this, as Februus lived with her tribe although separate and apart. But it was the first time the priest had verbally confirmed this to her or anyone in her village for she would have heard about it. The Twelve Elders was the stuff of legends and it was dangerous information at that. If you believed the stories about the Twelve, they each had great knowledge and therefore power. There were many people that would torture, kill, and destroy to extract what each of the Twelve knew and use it for their own ends.

So long ago, the Twelve dispersed and hid, taking their knowledge with them, keeping it safe. Until it was the right time to share it with the Remnant.

Em continued in her musings. So, all along in her little forsaken corner of the world, one of the twelve keepers of the Knowledge was hiding in plain sight. But if he was now sharing this dangerous information with them, it verified that this must be the time of revelation that was predicted for so long. Maybe now was the time for precious wisdom to be shared? Was this what her full mission was all about? Up to now she only knew parts.

Sitting with this uncomfortable insight brought goosebumps along her spine, as she sensed the hidden danger that this portended. Now she was quite glad that this had been hidden from her during her brief young life. Well, up until this point.

As if following the threads of Em's thoughts, Februus proceeded, "I have lived with Em's tribe on the Island of the Lady for a long time. Yet, my part in our great mission is coming to an end. I have been one of the Twelve Keepers of the lost knowledge, until it was time for it to be shared with the world again. Brave you have been given an object to protect and deliver by your tribe's Elder as your mission. Is it not true?"

Brave nodded, as he was surprised again. He returned to the annoying thought that everyone else seemed to know what he was expected to do except for him.    And this man was close to terrifying as he could walk among others' thoughts.    He was operating on another level.

However, Brave knew he could also trust him. He could feel the Priest's beneficial energy pulsing inside of the cave like a heartbeat.    He also recalled his own village elder's directions to send him directly to Island of the Lady.    Everything was mysteriously as it was foretold.

In one fluid motion, Brave reached inside of his shirt.    He hooked the rough twine necklace with his thumb.    For a moment he drew it up into the flickering torchlight before letting it drop swiftly out of sight.

Brave noted with some frustration, "Yes. I keep this mysterious object close.    And I found the Island of the Lady, then Lady Liberty and Em.    That completes the first phase of my mission, which seemed difficult enough. All I know now is Em and I are supposed to take the object somewhere to unlock the stored knowledge within it. But who, where and what is beyond me."

Brave's voice had escalated as he ended this small speech, wavering with emotion.    Yet even while he was talking there were new thoughts walking through his mind.    Here he was standing in front of one of the Twelve!  If anyone could piece together the network of knowledge, it would have to be Februus!  That was their whole job wasn't it?

Fervently, Brave wished he had paid more attention to his Elder's stories now. Momentarily, he was a young boy again sitting in a circle of children around the old man's feet. He shook his head chastising himself. He could see his adolescent games with sticks and stones in the dirt only half listening to stories about what the Twelve's powerful minds could do. Now he felt quite unprepared as he felt the direct power of Februus' intellect patiently waiting for Brave's mind to catch up.

After a brief pause, Februus replied to Brave's internal questions,

"Yes, as one the Twelve I've been one of the keepers of knowledge too. But I am only one, and my time is swiftly coming to a close."

He held up a matching small metal object like the one nestled in the pouch close to Brave's heart. However, Februus' object was tinted a deep blue. Brave's piece was more of an amethyst. As he continued to speak, he placed the sacred object in a small pouch strung with a more finely tooled leather thong necklace. He continued his monologue as he performed several symbolic hand rituals over the metal object.

"I've lived many generations on this Earth keeping the knowledge safe until it was time to pass it into the right hands. That time is now. Long ago, the Twelve of us Elders perfected a few methods for us to communicate with each other even though we have lived apart for an aeon of time. Brave your keeper died before you were born, which was a little problematic. We had to wait for you to grow up so there was a bit of a gap. My time is coming soon. I have kept myself alive using a few ancient methods. But, by exercising so much mental energy daily, I have placed heavy demands on my human vessel. It is time soon for me to return to the space in between."

Turning to Em he solemnly placed the pouch around her neck as he continued to speak, "Now the two of you have two of the twelve missing pieces to rebuild the hidden network of knowledge from our ancestors. All twelve need to be brought together again to grant complete access to our heritage."

"However, we are at a different point in the history of this planet. There have always been twelve paths to knowledge and only twelve. Even when someone thought they were forming a new religion or a new belief system it still could be categorized under one of the original twelve paths. We still know and practice some of the old names like Physics, Yoga, Buddhism, Mathematics or Christianity. Each of our twelve paths had lots of rigorous rules and requirements for that belief system to work. They would work but only if you did exactly what your teacher taught you. Also, all these twelve paths had something in common, they were considered masculine in energetic form. Very structured."

With a pause for breath, the priest turned to face Em. His glittering blue eyes were hypnotic. Quietly he continued,

"And as we know Em is of the tribe named Path. Path is a very symbolic, important name. For over the last few centuries they have been forging a new Path, the Thirteenth Path. They didn't necessarily know that as they are tucked in here out of the way with the Lady Liberty as their guardian."

As he spoke, Em sucked in her breath with a quick inhale. Here she thought she had been guarding the statue, but the priest was reversing their roles and turning everything upside down.

Februus resumed, "Yes this powerful symbol was infusing feminine energy into your Tribe. And now for the first time in human history, we are ready to launch people on the Thirteenth Path, which is energetically feminine in nature. Therefore, the Thirteenth is more in tune with Earth which is a feminine planet that compliments and works with the Sun's masculine energy. It is time. But the part that is the most mysterious about the Thirteenth Path is that all of the rules of the previous Twelve don't apply."

What was this man talking about? Em and Brave threw each other questioning glances. How can rules suddenly not apply?

With an abrupt turn towards Brave, Februus carried on with that fierce blue stare, "So Brave, it is innately easier for Em as a woman to follow this new feminine Path. She will guide you to the right destination for you two are now a partnership. Neither of you will succeed in your charged mission without the other. Always remember that. Brave you are the Messenger but Em is your Path that your message must follow. Sometimes this will feel awkward and quite difficult, for it is the exact opposite how this planet has always operated. This is the hinge of history, where finally the male and female energy is working in fluid tandem. You must trust her implicitly for this isn't just about the two of you, it is about humanity's future survival."

Then Brave said simply what he had already secretly told himself, "I will follow her anywhere."

With that Februus turned and led them back towards a firelit hearth.

"Come, there are a few more things we must do in order to properly prepare you for your journey."

# FEBRUUS AS THE MUSE

*The Spaces in Between the Stars*

With a breathless burst of light, a spark of soul burst into Darius' alcove study just off The Tapestry Room. Before this new arrival Darius already had company. It was Februus in spirit, still sporting some vestiges of his human form. He enjoyed his blue-eyes and orangey gold hair, he felt like a sunbeam from one of Earth's amazing sunsets.

Februus was an old soul like Darius. They had worked on numerous creative Universes, but none as unique as Earth. Many times, the pair second guessed themselves for investing so much into this Free Will experimental Universe. What were they thinking? So many eternal souls tuned to the Divine Source here in the Ether would fall apart once they got down into the muddiness of the clay. The physical distractions of Earth were so enticing. In each incarnation, they would surrender their Divine connection to perfect love. Then they would return to the spaces in between and beg for a redemptive rerun, only to fail miserably again. However, if and when a Soul finally did manage to overcome, it was the most powerful energy unleashed into the Universes ever witnessed.

For example, there were whole new worlds functioning in multiple dimensions that were created by the sacrifice of the Christ at his chosen crucifixion. But most souls were not functioning at that highest of levels, and then it was complete downhill once they entered Earth's Free Will state and intense physicality. It did not help that there were dark overlords creating sparkling deceptions as well. So that is how Darius and Februus worked up another plan of 3D support.

Darius recruited the Twelve Elders to reunite on Earth, Februus being one of the twelve. They did not incarnate anymore, that was long over for all of them. But after consulting with those closer to the Divine Source, Darius was given special dispensation to send the Twelve to Earth yet again. They could go in their Spirit forms and just cloak themselves in an optimal human disguise suited for a long journey. The Twelve could then function as indirect helpers of humanity without terrorizing the general population.

In this way they could retain their true consciousness of Spirit. Their eternal memories would not be suppressed like incarnating souls choosing life on Earth. Therefore, the Twelve Elders were also exempt from the restraining wheel of karma or the shackles of sin, whatever a human chose to call the limitations of the Game. They could help and assist but they were not allowed to unduly influence an outcome. It was a fine line that could not be crossed, or it would break the rules of a Free Will planet. And that was a whole other set of problems.

At the beginning of the homo sapien root race, these Twelve Souls incarnated to Earth and taught the latest birthed version of humanity many things including the contrivance of time.

When the Earth shifted and created four seasons from the more ancient two seasons, they devised the twelve-month calendar to help the humans farm to thrive instead of just survive. Each of the Twelve Elders were associated with one month of the newly formed calendar year.

Janus was assigned to January, Februus to February and Martius to March and so forth. The Elders were the equivalent of triathletes. They could run forever and were built for longevity. When on Earth, they were playing for the whole marble, angst over short term setbacks were ridiculous as small battles were only trivial. By the time Februus met Brave on the Island of the Lady, he had lived close to one millennia or a thousand years. Em and Brave were his last Earthly project before his cosmic final departure.

At this point however Februus returned for a brief celestial visitation with Darius. It must be serious if Darius summoned him to the space between the stars for this level of a meeting.

It was then that Februus recognized the sparkling soul that barged into his ponderous meeting with Darius. At first it looked like an invisible hand painting a holographic landscape into a corner of the room. Then the abstract streaks defined themselves into flowers. Finally, with a flourish, the sparkling diamond of a Sprinter soul flashed into its diaphanous form.

Sprinter souls were perfect complements to the Triathlete souls like the Twelve Elders who were best suited to long slogs in the muck. The marathoners did not move fast but they also could not be moved. Therefore, they could not easily be tempted to fall for distractions.

However, Darius also designed another soul adaptation perfect for Free Will planets struggling with repetitive karmic issues, the Sprinter soul. They were extraordinarily special for they committed to live very brief lives on Earth when it was called upon.

To combat Earth's deceptive entrapments, the Sprinters chose to live many short lives. Often, they impacted millions in their brief brilliance. But that influence came at the price of truncated lifespans, so that way fewer debts, sins or karma could be accumulated. It was a low risk, high reward scenario, well if you could disregard the pain upon each death.

This Sprinter Soul was slowly revolving in her sparkling beauty before the two hulking spirits of Darius and Februus as she acclimated to the other side. There was a pink feminine luster to many of the diamonds sprinkling the vision she projected as her cloak.

The most well-known life she had lived was as Joan of Arc. Her specialization was delivering game-changing messages from the Spirit Side of the veil to humanity. As in the case of Joan of Arc, her delivery often got her killed. After that important incarnation she was always known as Joan, even here on the Spirit side, which means approximately "God is gracious".

Other times she had chosen lives as a child betrayed by compromised adults around them. Her goal in those lives was to shine the powerful spotlight of Love to help weaker souls wake up faster, to start making better choices in their human lives and stop perpetrating pain on other humans. And as The Christ said, "A little child shall lead them..."

Joan was here to discuss her current incarnation as Janette the Parisian Femme-Artiste with Februus and Darius. Another pivotal brief shining life. There was an important message the two Elders were attempting to deliver to Janette that kept getting lost in Earthly translation.

They wanted Janette to plant some signposts particularly in her art for others to find in the future timelines. Jan-Waara and Shevanon were going to need confirmations from the past as they moved along their important missions in their future lives.

There were other messages being implanted and left particularly inside of Jan and Shev's DNA strands, the secret within. But they needed some insurance policies in case the duo did not exercise their skills to access this interior messaging system.

The mistranslations were happening because Joan's Sprinter life as Janette the French artist was coming to an end. She was secretly suffering from Tuberculosis and her lungs were not pumping enough oxygen anymore. Janette was driven by her divine purpose to encode divine messages into her calendar series. She now had *Janus*, *Februus* and *Martius* completed. But she wanted all Twelve done before her young body let her go.

Free of her physical malady while visiting in spirit, she did a joyous pirouette. On her last spin, she presented Februus with a holographic image of the Impressionist painting of *Februus* that she painted as Janette at her garret easel among the Laurent's rafters.

"Februus, you were a wonderful Muse, I must say!" Janette laughed. He was caught off guard for not only had she captured the riot of sunset colors found in the Earthly Februus' garb of fiery hair and cornflower blue eyes, but the brushy outline of a faun was also evident. The faun was Februus' favorite disguise as a mythical creature roaming the world's forests, making many humans question everything about their existence. Which was of course exactly Februus' point. Question everything, and you might surprise yourself and birth a new reality while you are at it.

Before she left Darius' oasis, she relaxed into a meditative state. This allowed for an easier activation and download of a batch of conceptual numbers, letters, and sacred geometry into the sleeping vehicle of Janette. Having Joan's full source here with them created a cleaner transmission of so much information.

Numbers and shapes have many layers of meaning embedded into them. Words are abstracts that can distract in soul downloads. They decided to include a forgiveness matrix:

318

91K6

231

It looked random but there was deep meaning. Meditating on this combination sets a frequency for New Harmony. The interesting thing that they had discovered was that the matrix was still activated even when invisible to the naked eye. If Janette inserted it under the paint, it was still functioning divinely influencing the eye of the beholder.

They had discovered this artistic application with Leonardo da Vinci, he had all kinds of secret codes in his works. It was an important reason why they resonated.

Back in Paris, when Janette woke up, she would recall and trust the abstract information more, due to her soul's visit while asleep. Janette would embed it under the riot of colorful paints right where they belonged. Waiting to be found somewhere in the future if needed by Sean, Janice, Em or Brave. However the embedded codes would also set a New Harmony by whoever else viewed the paintings too.

The transmission was pitch perfect, so one more hurdle down in the mission to keep this human race expanding instead of collapsing. When Darius was alone again, he could not help but joke, "Oh, what tangled webs we weave," as he stared into the pulsing Tapestry representing all of humanity.

# RITES & RITUALS

*40.6895° N, 74.0449° W*
*The Caves on the Island of the Lady*

Februus led them to another area in the maze of cavernous chambers where there was a hot underground bubbling spring. There was a faint whiff of seashells in the air but not overwhelmingly so. As they walked Februus quietly spoke,

"Long ago, each of the twelve Elders were named based on their responsibilities and, also for a month of the year. I was named after Februus, the Roman god. He presided over the Roman purification ritual celebrated on the fifteenth day of February. The month was named after this ritual and presiding god. In their ancient calendar, March was the first month of the year as it was the Spring Equinox. Therefore, February was the Omega closing out each year."

"The Romans were a warring nation. The cleansing rituals were embedded in their culture with large, scaled bath houses. To purify and cleanse in preparation and in absolution upon their return from battle."

This was new territory for Brave, in that he remembered truly little of the scraps of ancient history taught by his tribe. It seemed pointless information, as those dead were all gone. Vaguely, he recalled the names of the months that came from a lost civilization.

They approached some private spaces where Februus had prepared towels and robes for each of them, so they could enter the springs and bathe.

The water felt quite buoyant. It must be loaded with salt for they kept floating up to the surface. It was so peaceful and primal at the same time. In the deep gloaming lights, they could hear Februus' resonant pleasant voice speaking to them over the water.

"This time has been foretold. I have waited so long to complete my duties as Februus. I wasn't sure if it was ever going to come." He said with a gentle smile, "But now the Messenger and the Path are together at last."

"I am fulfilling some of my last responsibilities in this role. We will start your joined journey with this ancient purification ritual. When you feel refreshed, come join me again in front of the fire for there are a few more important messages that I must share with you before your departure. Take your time, there is no rush. Spend the time you require in these healing waters, so your bodies are replenished with any minerals they might be lacking."

Februus, left them as he walked away down the shadowy halls. Leaving the trail of torchlights for them to follow. Suddenly, both Em and Brave were self-conscious, finding themselves alone, floating in these sensuous waters.

"I guess we are departing," Brave said with a raised eyebrow and a crooked grin, "Sure glad I'm only the Messenger and not the one figuring out our Path. So where are we going?"

Brave could feel more than see her inscrutable smile playing across those voluptuous lips in the deep shadows. Staying true to her reticent nature, Em replied, "Far."

With that Brave could resist her no longer. The semi-darkness gave him brevity he so needed with this mysterious young woman. He gently placed one hand on her shoulder and the other on the back of her head, tipping those generous lips to his mouth. Sharing his amour without speaking one word.

# RIDDLE SOLVED

*39.7447° N, 75.5484° W*
*Wilmington, Delaware 2000s*

Sean ran his burly hand over his wife's olive skin as she
slept next to him. He murmured softly into her hair
so she could not hear:

"Days were islands I traveled along, one at a time
down a chain to the sea…"

Janice expanded his creative side. He swore she changed
his brain chemistry bringing lines of poetry to the tip of
his tongue.

"…the sun reflects back and laughs at my song,
until finally, finally I found thee."

Janice stirred under his touch turning with sleepy eyes
gazing into his loving stare. Around the board room,
Sean could be quite daunting. His resonant voice and
steely resolve got a lot of decisions made by the sheer
force of his will. But here, behind closed doors with
Janice, he was another man altogether. A better one at
that.

Abruptly Sean stated, "I like myself better with you," causing Janice's sumptuous lips to thin out into a brilliant grin. He carried on, "So I want you to get ready. Because I have a surprise for you. We are going to Washington D.C. today. I think I have found the person to help solve your art puzzle. Well, at least provide you with another clue," he qualified.

Janice's eyes widened in shocked surprise. She had this way of lifting her eyelids up to prance along the top of her irises, but not quite enough to see the whites of her eye above them. It was quite alluring to Sean. But this time, Sean could see almost the whole whites of her eyes, so he knew that this was a great gift to her.

It had been a few months since their weekend in New York City, where they attended the lovely cocktail party hosted by Sir Andrew Featherstone.

Since that night, the obscure Februus painting had not left Janice's curious mind. As she often did, she soon made fast friends with Sir Andrew that evening. Immediately, they began to sleuth away to identify this unknown artist. Who was this J. Laurent? Was it a nom de plume for a famous artist that wanted to try out a new Impressionist breaststroke?

Janice loved puzzles. Through email, Janice and the art collector shared notes and ideas. So far, they traced the painting back to the famed art broker, Monsieur Durand-Ruel, who could be credited with at least partially launching the fledgling Impressionists through his support. Then an English bibliophile allowed Sir Andrew to review the books he had purchased from Durand-Ruel's estate. He had ledgers and bills of sale from the ancient art house in his collection.

In the deceased's books and records was found the bill of lading for the original purchase of the *Februus* conveying the painting to its original owner! But there was still no record of the artist.

The fabled art dealer kept meticulous records of his artists and was known to be fair and generous in payment. He was not one to financially abuse an artist in his stable. So why was there no ledger for payments made to an artist named J. Laurent? It was there, the mystery stalled, until now.

By this time Janice was on her knees bouncing up and down on the bed, which made for an amazing vision of motion as they preferred to sleep in the nude. With complete disregard, Janice's hands were locked in prayer.

"What? What? Please! What?" She was laughing like a little girl at a birthday party. Again, Sean marveled at this complicated woman he had married, and would kill for. Expensive jewelry never got this kind of reaction, she loved them and wore each and everyone but there was no jumping up and down on the bed. He was beginning to unravel her mind, understanding that the solving of an enigma was her greatest exhilaration.

Laughing, and fending her knees off his belly, Sean replied, "Yes, get up and get dressed. For we must make the train in an hour for Washington. We have an appointment with an associate at the Smithsonian Institute. He has located a collection of Durand-Ruel's personal correspondence, and he has it at our disposal."

"What!" Like a flash Janice bounded naked from their bed and had disappeared into the closet, where a flurry of hangars and clothes began to be tossed about in a mad fury. Sean thought to himself, "Whenever will I learn to make afternoon appointments?" He must be mad to be driving his riveting woman from their bed. He never could get enough of times like this."

# MORE INSTRUCTIONS

*40.6895° N, 74.0449° W*
*The caverns of the Island of the Lady, 2500s*

When they returned to the hearth, the pair was refreshed but they were also united in purpose. Februus was seated in front of a simple round table and had a few items arranged on the roughly hewn planks. As he motioned for them to join him, Brave could feel his great mind at work. It must have been something about being underground. Maybe the rocks shut out energy from other objects and people? Brave was not sure, but it was intense, like a sunbeam's shaft lighting up a darkened room.

This was an intellect at a level he had never encountered before. It gave him a small feeling of comfort in the pit of his belly as well as gratitude that there were these sentinel great beings guarding sacred knowledge for the sake of humanity. But then he was also quite sorrowful that Februus appeared to be prophesying his own coming demise. How could it be possible that his role was near completion? There was so much inside of this great teacher that would be lost, Brave could just intuitively sense it.

The firelight glistened on Februus' pale features and bearded face, and it was clear that he was reading the thoughts of both young people. That was frustrating to Brave, for Em's mind was an enigma separate and apart from himself. In a flash, he was envious of Februus' effortless ability to stroll through her thoughts.

Februus began his instruction, "Much I have to share will be strange to you, and really our basic language is not robust enough to clearly convey these deeper meanings. Therefore, it is best if I simply download into your minds symbols and images that are important for you to permanently retain."

With that a picture of what looked like a coiled messy rope appeared in the front of their minds. It was folded onto itself over and over, but not in an organized fashion. When one looked closely at the skein it was also twisted. It looked something like a rope ladder that was twirled around and around without any of the rungs breaking. But the folds were incredibly complex creating fantastical twists and turns in and of themselves. As their minds' eyes were drawn deeper and deeper into the beautiful minute details of the object, they saw what looked like flashes of light jumping across the layers, like lightning across the sky.

Brave could hear Em's quick inhale of breath as her eyes glistened quickly with tears over the beauty that they were both witnessing in their minds. And for the first time, Brave could feel her elusive thoughts, somehow Februus was creating a mental bridge for the two of them to share.

On each rung of the ladders were tiny blips. They looked like smooth stones in a stream, cresting above the water, but too numerous to count. As they looked closely at these tiny details, every blip was unique. There was an infinite range in hues and shapes.

As they were mentally drawn into the image, it was as if they were now flying or swimming between the rungs of the twisted rope ladders, piled up in this chaotic yet joyous conflagration. This must be what birds feel like Brave thought to himself as he flew between the empty spaces. It was like an elegant Universe in and of itself. One could only say, it felt alive.

There was this underlying pulsating glow of energy pumping from every aspect of this entangled ladder of light. They began to feel and hear a ringing vibration throughout their bodies. Also, the entangled chaotic mass seemed to vibrate at one musical note, like a tuning fork. It would ring to a feverish pitch then recede, and then begin to ascend in force all over again, but always on the same note. As their bodies sped up in flight, they could hear the faint sound of the most angelic music, and this structure was sounding only one note of the musical score. They were immersed in a full-bodied sensory experience. This felt like the epitome of love.

After some time, the young couple could hear Februus' voice calling them back into the physical, but they did not want to leave this fantastic, beautiful world. They could hear him coaxing them to return, noting that this image would now always be within them, they could return at any time for sustenance.

With a jolt they snapped back into their bodies, leaving them both shaking their heads in wonderment. The colors and the sounds in their altered state were so rich in texture and depth compared to their physical surroundings, even Februus' head of fiery hair. In fact, reality now felt somewhat drab in comparison. It made Brave question if Reality was not as real as he had always assumed.

Now it seemed easier to dialogue with Februus on a mental level. Words were not, as necessary. Therefore, Februus' explanation of what they experienced was partially verbal, but also inside of their heads. After a quiet pause, Februus spoke words of wisdom that made their ears vibrate.

"That ringing in your ears is your own body's recognition when it hears and feels the truth. As you know your body is made up of trillions of cells, like the stars in the sky. The image that you saw in your mind's eye was a picture of the complex Universe inside each of your cells!"

"Now I am telling you what intuitively you already know, but it has been lost in the human records of time. This is valuable information, some of which has been recorded on the metal objects that each of you now carry. Hundreds of years ago scientists were studying our cells and made many discoveries. They nicknamed the microscopic material in each cell DNA."

"However, I will tell you a secret. Everything recorded on these objects is already embedded in your DNA. For as you saw with your own eyes it is multi-dimensional and therefore informational. It defies our physical reality of chemistry and science. It is a gateway to higher consciousness here in the physical. But it is also a gateway to the Other Side. The difficulty is most humans have lost their way and no longer know how to access all knowledge from within. In fact, for thousands of years, one small group practiced downright suppression of this access to amass power and wealth for a few. They erroneously believed that there was a finite supply. Coupled with their thirst for power and domination, they failed to accept that they were choosing a path of destruction for all."

As Februus was instructing them, the beautiful cellular image was rotating inside of their minds so they could continue to view its awesome complexity.

"The more our scientific ancestors experimented they wanted to quantify it here in what they coined 3D reality. But you can see from your own experience that the 3D is dull compared to the space in between. They were trying to apply 3D physical logic to a higher dimension. They needed to be outside the system."

Quietly Februus paused. "Now, you have experienced what it is like to be outside the 3D system. Now you know the awesome power that exists in each one of us at our cellular level. Ancient scientists were getting at the power of our cellular model when they were discussing entanglement theory. And it scared them. For they liked to be the intelligentsia with the masses reliant on them. What would happen if people began to realize the power that laid inside each and every one of them? The elite's discovery terrified them, for it threatened their power structure and exposed their own future irrelevancy."

"Inside of you Brave, inside of you Em, and every person has their own DNA print unique to them. Each human's blueprint is replicated trillions of times across every cell in their own body. So, your body literally sings out to you, it is a beautiful instrument, and you are its conductor whether you know it or not."

"I've spent many years as a recluse here in these caves for a number of reasons. But one outcome is I have activated much of my cellular structure. That is why I can talk to you inside of your minds among other things. To use the slang, I know how to get on your wavelength. In 3D terms, I operate at about 60% of my capacity. When we think on the ancient Jesus Christ, he was at 100%. There were others like the Buddha, Gandhi that were at high levels too. That is why we still know of them today, for they achieved something we know we are missing."

"However, I have also worn this physical body down, as I have brought so much energy through this vehicle. It is time for me to leave this frame soon and return to the Space in Between. It has been calling my name for a while. As I said before, it is important for me to help you both access information stored in your multi-dimensional DNA. Remember the two objects you carry are only backups of what we all carry within. They are only a roadmap to help humans regain access to all the knowledge buried inside of each one of us. It is time for humans to return to their full glory."

Februus' glistening cornflower blue eyes bored into Em's for a moment, filled with filial love.

"You my dear child will need to be the leader in these matters. For your Tribe of the Path were planted here with me and the Lady for a reason. You have been energetically working this internal path and have built up some capacity. Brave lost access to the Twelve's teachings when his Elder, one of the Twelve, left Earth before Brave's birth. So, Brave has not had the same time to access more capacity. Brave will follow your path." Februus smiled at his own small joke."

# SMITHSONIAN SLEUTHING

*38.9072° N, 77.0369° W*
*Washington, D.C. 2000s*

Janice and Sean sat down across the laboratory table from Mr. Pettit, the Smithsonian archivist who was Sean's contact. Between them was a computer screen digitally displaying some handwritten correspondence between Durand Ruel and the mysterious J. Laurent! After introductions, Mr. Pettit began to explain how he knew Sean, as business executives and reclusive archivists did not normally run in the same circles.

He cleared his throat, as he fidgeted with his tie, "It was the restoration project of Lady Liberty. That is how Sean and I first met. Sean was our point of contact at the company which committed the gold to restore the flame of the torch. We had in our archives some manuscripts from a master guild on the ancient process of gold leaf application. Often the old ways are the best, as was the case here. We were happy to be a part of that amazing worldwide collaboration."

Janice glanced at Sean, her face glowing with pride, as she squeezed his burly hand under the table. So many complex layers to this man she thought privately to herself.

Mr. Pettit proceeded, "As you can imagine the Smithsonian's collections are vast, and we are still getting a handle on developing more robust search tools in our databases. Donated batches of personal correspondence from people's estates are still a weak spot in our archive system. So, when Sean called me about your successful sleuthing so far, I wasn't too confident I could pinpoint anything further in the literal sea of paper surrounding us."

Again, the man nervously clawed at his throat, shaking his head as if to clear his thoughts. Janice thought to herself that he must be quite an anxious personality based on this nervous tic. However, Janice was unaware of the impact she often had on men. There were many women that were classically more beautiful than she. But there was something enigmatically appealing in Janice's eyes. She also emanated a magnetic energy that made some people quite nervous, as was the case here with Mr. Pettit. But it was what Sean secretly loved about her the most. For he would come home after a long tiresome day, and he would feel these waves of energy washing over him, healing all the wounds he had suffered that day.

Mr. Pettit seemed to be finding words to string together again, as he recovered from the Janice Effect. This was Sean's secret designation for his wife's impact on other men. Sean found it funny that Janice really had no idea that she was often the cause of powerful, proud men suddenly bumbling into unsure schoolboys. She misread these episodes as a dislike of her or a nervous tic as in this case.

"At first I was just plugging in search strings into different databases and not getting anywhere too fast. But then an idea just popped into my head. I remembered the research I had done for Sean on the Lady Liberty project. There was some connection between a French family and Bartholdi, the sculptor. The Laurent name sounded familiar to me. Could J. Laurent be that same family? And Voila! It was!"

With a flair he turned to the screen and started expanding boxes so they could read the scans of handwritten correspondence. The Institute had adopted a policy procedure of preservation for old correspondence. After exposing the document to one scan, they secured them in temperature-controlled vaults. Then they worked from the scans, as much as possible.

Apparently, the Laurent family had hosted a dinner party where Bartholdi, the Statue of Liberty's sculptor, Eiffel, and Durand Ruel were all in attendance! They only knew this, as this batch of personal letters included thank-you letters to the Laurent family for a scintillating evening of friendship and discussion.

It was interesting to discover different pertinent facts from Bartholdi and Durand Ruel's letters. However, it was the latter's letters that held the smoking gun! Janette, the Laurent's genteel daughter, was the artist! As a young eligible lady of her day, it was not seemly for her to be in any trade as it would jeopardize her chance at a marriage match.

So, her father was her cover, and Janette was "off the books"! That was why there was no paper trail or documentation for Janette's work. Mr. Pettit had also discovered that she had painted a sister painting called *Martius*, the Roman word for March which was the first month in the Roman calendar. Martius was the month to honor their Roman god, Mars, the god of war and a protector of Rome. The Romans were great at acquiring others' cultures. They had relied heavily on the Greek lexicon of gods and goddesses when they conquered their neighbor's older culture. In the Greek tradition Mars, the god of war, was known as Ares.

As it often is, when one mystery is solved, it only leads to another. Janice began daydreaming about what the *Martius* painting would look like compared to the peaceful *Februus* painting. It must be a study in contrasts if Janette was staying true to the concept of a warring Mars. It was almost as if she could see it in her mind's eye, hauntingly familiar, but just out of reach. She wondered what this young girl's life must have been like, born into a different age. As Janice returned from her inner musings, she realized Sean and Mr. Pettit were beginning a startling new line of conversation.

Obliquely, the archivist asked Sean, "Should I proceed?"

Gravely, Sean turned and looked directly into his wife's eyes. "What you feel appropriate to share with me goes for Janice as well. You can think of us as one. We will keep this conversation between ourselves, until you tell us otherwise."

Janice thought, whatever could they be talking about? It sounded like a spy movie where everyone was talking in double speak. With a deep inhale Mr. Pettit began his strange tale.

# SLEEP ON IT

*40.6895° N, 74.0449° W*
*The caves on the Island of the Lady, 2500s*

Februus left Brave and Em for his own sleeping quarters in a nearby corridor. With the use of animal skins and woven blankets, Februus had made this corner of the underground catacombs quite cozy instead of the expected dampness. His last words were somewhat mysterious even though quite simple in direction.

"It is best for you both to stay here with me tonight in the caves to sleep and ponder on these things I have shown you today. It will help cement your mental connection so you can grow your new skills of speaking mind to mind. The rocks are also sentient beings and will help direct your minds' energies. And this new skill will be an important tool for you to wield."

They were quite snug in their makeshift bed of animal skins, and they were both quite drowsy from their full day of mental adventures with Februus. Brave rolled onto his left side so he could gaze into Em's unfathomable eyes as he reached and cradled her hands in his. There must be something to it about these rocks, for the air was almost vibrating with energy around them. It was difficult to keep their eyes open, as sleep pulled them down the tunnel again, but this time they walked hand in hand.

In their collaborative dream, they stepped down the same staircase they walked earlier that day. As they reached the bottom of the stairs, there was now water lapping their feet as they were suddenly walking along a shoreline with a band of other warriors. There was a young girl in the center that they all encircled protectively. Em had an arrow drawn tautly on a bow as she circled around to the back of the group pointing her arrow upwards into the sky at an invisible foe.

Brave found himself on the right flank of the group with a sword drawn from its sheath. There was a power emanating in invisible waves from the little girl as she skipped through the surf, singing rhymes to herself. She seemed oblivious to her protective detail around her, as if she were used to this arrangement.

They finally found what the group seemed to be searching for, it was a wooden post sticking out of the waves. As they grasped the post one by one nothing happened. However, upon the girl's touch, a stone's throw away from the group, a doorway magically appeared as a gateway to nowhere. It was made of three monolithic stones. When you looked through the space, all you saw was more ocean all the way to the horizon. It did not look any different from the view on either side of the stone frame. But Brave intuitively knew that it was somehow a portal to another dimensional space or world. A shortcut, in essence, if you were courageous enough to walk through to the other side. He thought to himself, how powerfully in touch with the Great Spirit this young girl must be if she could achieve what none of the warriors could.

Suddenly everything was a jumble, arrows seemed to be flying through the portal right at them from the other side! Immediately, the front line raised their shields to protect the young girl, who seemed to be the target of these invisible foes.

The slip of a girl began to run fearlessly towards the opening looking to crossover, as if she believed she was invincible. With a shout, the leader of the band, starting yelling,

"Keep her back! It is not safe yet! Keep her here, crossover first and prepare the way. We cannot risk it."
"Martius, I AM ready! I've been preparing for this for a long time!" she yelled back at him.

While this argument continued, a smaller posse broke off including Brave and Em as if this was part of a previously planned foray. They began charging through the surf towards the portal with shields extended and weapons drawn. With a crash they breached the mystical doorway.

At this moment, Brave could feel a surge of power lifting his team up as if they were entering an invisible current coursing up into the heavens. As he looked downward to the shoreline quickly disappearing, he could see their young ward wading through the crashing waves, now chest high. She had her right arm raised above her head, waving, waving. The portal had closed upon their entry leaving the rest of their posse who remained to protect their young charge.

Brave could hear her tearful cries over the rough surf, as she waved up into the sky, apparently frustrated by their protective betrayal to leave her behind.

"You were supposed to take me through! I'm ready!"

Then Brave descended deeper into Morpheus' dreamless abyss. He slumbered and remembered no more.

# GIGANTIC TALES

*38.9072° N, 77.0369° W*
*Washington, D.C. 2000s*

Turning to Janice, Mr. Pettit stated, "First of all, please call me Ethan. What I am about to share with you is an institutional secret I stumbled upon by accident. I was not in the need-to-know group, so if it is ever discovered that I gained access to this information, I would probably be fired from my position and subsequently defamed if I spoke out. But the stories are beginning to leak out, so I think it is important for some outsiders to know the truth, now before it is spun in the national news stories."

Janice murmured, "Kind of like an insurance policy."

"Exactly," Ethan agreed. "There really is no way to explain this, so I'm just going to say it. For over a hundred years, the Smithsonian has gathered up old skeletons found across America and quietly stored them away. Now, you might ask, why and if true, why don't we ever see them on display? Well, the truth is quite shocking. We now have thousands and thousands of them. And guess what, they are all giants!"

Eyes round, the couple's jaws literally hung slack in complete surprise.

Ethan bravely carried on changing their world view with every word, "They average around eight feet tall, some as tall as ten feet. Obviously, their massive scale and quantity of remains do not fit the current scientific narrative that has been preached as dogma for close to a hundred years. It calls into questions our presumptive assumption that we moderns are the apex of human history. Sadly, this goes back to the belief system cobbled together by our grand institution's founder, a product of his times, where many believed that the Europeans were intellectually superior to the natives found in the Americas."

"But the appalling new trust was not just about intellect and human size, it was also about the age of the find. We have been carbon dating these bones for a long, long time. And no one wants to speak the truth. Because no matter what the scientists do, the bones test as ancient. Way beyond the current Clovis-First theory, which is the mainstream scientific dogmatic belief which states that the Americas were empty until ten thousand years ago, when the first Native American tribes immigrated here. A lot of academic works would be discarded if this more ancient timeline were accepted. It is hard for scientists to admit that a major presumption has been horribly wrong for a long time!"

Ethan had paused after ending in almost a shout of frustration. Now that he had broken his code of secrecy, it was like a confession. He could not stop letting the truth flow freely.

"One of the alternative ways that I began to fact check these jarring discoveries was by reading Native American oral traditions that were recorded by missionaries and historians. Apparently, when we first arrived in America from Europe, the tribal leaders all told the same story. There was an ancient race that was here long before them. Some of them were white skinned with blonde and red hair. And they were giants. They had double rows of teeth that were of a stronger substance than ours not subject to decay. The Indian tribes called them the Mound Builders, for they built these huge earthen works across the land. They worshipped the union of Earth and sky by designing these mounds to match important astrological alignments, just like the pyramid and stone-henge builders did on other continents. The Mound Builders also honored their dead by burying them inside of these earthen mounds, layers upon layers of them."

Ethan paused to take a sip of water. There was dead silence in the room, as Sean and Janice were rendered speechless. Where did one even begin? Ethan plowed in again:

"Of course, our European ancestors dismissed these recollections, as it was diametrically opposed to their world view. However, as time went by the agrarian society that America was becoming began to bring these secret truths literally to the surface. This is when I turned to our newspaper archive, which I am grateful to say has a much better roadmap of search keys for easier research than our personal correspondence database. You wonder how government funding can be so misspent?" Ethan muttered more to himself before continuing his riveting strange trail.

"As farmers began to till new fields across this great land, they began to make discovery after discovery of ancient Indian burial mounds. Starting with the Civil War there was an agrarian surge as people started over again, and this was in alignment with a string of newspaper printing presses popping up in every small town. So, you can imagine my surprise, when I queried words like 'giant, skeletons, Indian, burial mounds' what I found. There were hundreds and thousands of newspaper articles beginning in the 1860's up until the present documenting thousands of discoveries of these ancient remains. From Catalina Island in California to the Great Plains, the swamps in Florida, the Northeast. Basically everywhere," Ethan paused quietly.

Bravely he continued with his lower lip beginning to tremble and his eyes lowered in shame. "I was in shock. How could this be? This changed everything, why wasn't my great institution at the forefront of sharing this game changing knowledge? But that was not the worst part of it. In so many of the articles, there was one chilling phrase. Every article ended with a comment that a scientist from the Smithsonian Institute appeared and took the giant skeletons away for further research. Fast forward to today. So where are all the bones? Where is all the research? You can imagine my shock and dismay, when I came to realize that my whole proud career at this great institution was tainted by possibly one of the greatest cover-ups in modern science. It is not right. We all deserve to know the truth. It is time."

Still Ethan's two listeners were staggering under the portent of his words. Ethan's chin sagged down into his cupped hand, as he propped his elbow up on the table. His fingers on his other hand drummed out a nervous staccato on the tabletop, as he debated on what to share next.

With sudden decisiveness, Ethan charged forward, "Sadly, I realized that the people keeping these discoveries quiet," at this point Ethan interrupted himself: "I refer to them as the Black Hats instead of the euphemistic They. The Black Hats were abusing a Public Law, NAGPRA, that was originally meant to provide protections to the descendants of Native Americans. NAGPRA stands for The Native American Graves Protection and Repatriation Act and it was codified in 1990. I told you how historically as well as currently, tribal leaders have been consistently clear that the Mound Builders were a separate ancient race that were dead long and gone before their arrival in the Americas. And apparently, in some of the DNA tests that I have secretly gained access to, this has been proven true. The giant skeletons share almost zero genetic markers with Native American DNA. I am certainly not a Carbon dating expert, as I work mostly with manuscripts, but it appears that our secret collection of giant skeletons date to a much older period, as in dinosaur times."

"WHAT?" Sean and Janice exploded simultaneously.

"I know this seems quite impossible to believe. You can imagine how people in powerful positions would lose a LOT of face if it came out that they could be so wrong for so long. But then you can understand how much worse it would be for the cover up itself to be discovered. It would drive the public trust of the entire scientific community into a state of question. So, the scientific community now hides behind NAGPRA stating that it is not safe to share this information as it would disrespect today's tribes, so they can keep the giants slumbering safe from prying public eyes."

Janice interjected, "So ironic, since the science itself proves that the ancient giant skeletons are in no way related to any of the tribes to which they are being attributed." After a brief pause, Janice blurted out, "So how can we help?"

This last query tumbling from Janice's sumptuous lips did not surprise Sean any longer. He had eventually come to love this jarring character trait of hers: jumping into the fray when a task seemed to border on the lands of the impossible. It was often unsettling where these adventures might lead them, but he had come to trust Janice's instinct to forge a new path when she appeared to be only using her considerable empathy as their primary compass.

In response, Sean leaned slightly into their conversation, quizzically lifting his left eyebrow. As if to embrace the concept of Janice's latest interest but also signaling the unspoken question, "How did we get here and where are we going?".

He managed many outcomes in boardrooms, not with a preponderance of words, but with the power of his persona and non-verbal shifts that migrated conversations in the direction he preferred. This character trait translated well into his personal life, for Janice was a force in nature that he could only meet square-on. Words often fled his thoughts when he dove into her loving gaze.

Returning to Janice's question that still lingered in the air, Ethan startled them yet again with a quick nod of the head,

"Well, why yes you actually can. Word needs to get outside the walls of academia for it will only be the light of day that sets these truths free. Having various people talking about it in different circles, will help get the word out. For those of us inside are being suppressed, or even worse," Ethan's last words were trailing off in a smaller voice more to himself. But Ethan's voice had trailed off again almost to a whisper as he finished that last train of thought. As he charged forward, his voice picked up some energy:

"In order for you to have credibility as a goodwill ambassador for the cause, you will need to do some homework and go see some evidence for yourselves. If you feel so inclined, visiting an archaeologist in the field working an active site would be a beneficial endeavor."

By this time, Sean could feel the excitement seeping from Janice's pores as she began to squirm in her seat in anticipation as they listened to Ethan's suggestion.

"Dr. Goodman is working on an active site called Topper, I believe. He serves in the Archaeology Department at the University of South Carolina. If I recall correctly, this site is located on the Savannah River. It was discovered when the specialty chemical plant that owns the land was getting ready to do an expansion."

Sean cleared his throat in a start of surprise. "Oh yes, I know them, Tar-Trex, for they are one of our customers. They have a process that extracts the pine tar from old tree stumps and repurposes it into resins and rosins used in a myriad of applications such as body lotion and hair products..."

Sean's voice trailed off as he wrapped his index finger around one stray curl escaping Janice's attempt at a sleek cosmopolitan hairstyle suitable in her mind for a trip to DC. However, the coiffe was not so suitable to Janice the pathfinder as it attempted to escape the confinement of bobby pins.

As he gently released the tendril of her hair he brusquely continued, "I was scheduled to visit them next quarter, but there is no time like the present. I do not see why I cannot arrange a field trip for our favorite Nancy Drew here to visit Mr. Goodman's archaeological dig to see some of these giants for herself. And what better place to discuss mysterious topics such as ancient giant skeletons then under the cover of a business meeting?" Ethan and Janice both smiled in agreement.

# SITTING AMONGST
# THE RAFTERS

*48.8566° N, 2.3522° E*
*Paris, France, 1870's*

J anette awoke to the sun's beams playing across her face. The palpable beauty of the sun's warmth was something she would never tire. With an urgency, she hurried into her robe and slippers and scurried up into her art studio tucked into their family home's attic.

She reached into the pocket of her bathrobe and pulled out the scrawled notes that she had written in the middle of the night. She had no idea what they meant but she knew it was important. As her lungs continued to fail her, the more clarity she seemed to have about things unseen. It was like she disconnected from her ailing physical body; the veil was lifting.

She lined up the empty canvases she had not started yet in the remainder of her Calendar Series. With a pencil she began to sketch in order the numbers and letters that she had scribbled through the night. It was a compulsion that did not make any sense. But she knew it was some message coming through her not from her.

318

91K6

231

Whatever it meant, it felt good just looking at the seemingly random arrangement. As she sketched, Janette began to hum deep in her throat. Mirroring the purrs of her cat curled up on the window seat cushion, lapping up more solar bars of butter.

She vowed to herself yet again that she would finish as many of these twelve paintings as she could before her afflicted lungs permanently failed her. The art would be her living legacy. If only she could keep her Mother at bay just a little longer before her maternal antennae warned her that there was something deeply amiss. Janette knew there was no motherly fixing that could heal her lungs, so she jealously guarded the small allotment of time she had left to send her artful messages into the future.

# TAKING COLA BY STORM

*34.0007° N, 81.0348° W*
*Columbia, South Carolina, 2000s*

Sean and Janice arrived in the capitol city's lovely little airport. The locals lovingly foreshortened its name to Cola, combining the first three letters with the last. There was even a restaurant bearing the moniker. The company's jet glided to a stop, and in a few moments, they were whisked away by a driver of a local private car company. Sean's business life was seamlessly managed by Linda, his executive assistant located at their Delaware based headquarters. She meticulously planned each step of Sean's corporate travel, leaving nothing to chance.

However, events do not always go according to plan. Professor Goodman had returned from the field to the classroom. There was a graduate seminar which he was leading this week. The University of South Carolina's main campus was nestled around the proud state's Capitol building right in the center of the city. Therefore, Sean dropped Janice off in the historical heart of the campus before he continued to his final destination of his customer's plant. This was not the first time Janice had walked across the leafy green Horseshoe of Sean's alma mater. But each time she did she was touched by the timeless beauty of the place. It reminded her of those idyllic scenes in The Beautiful Mind movie and people strolling around on Princeton's lush lawns.

At first Janice was disappointed in this change of location, as she wanted to see the scientific site itself with the hopes of seeing ancient giant skeleton bones sticking out of the dirt. Her active imagination had already amused itself with dressing her up as the female Indiana Jones. After returning to Earth, she realized that there were many questions she wanted to ask the excavating academic. The silver lining in her cloud of disappointment may very well be that she could pepper her target with a lot more questions. She found it amusing how often men could not answer questions and do other tasks with their hands at the same time. On the flipside they were often downright brilliant when they could focus on the singular task at hand. Often, Sean took her breath away when she watched him in what she called "business mode". There was a glitter in his eye when he was over his target, to borrow one of his favorite phrases.

So, in preparation for her revised meeting with the scientist, she added another page of queries. She wanted to ensure she did not run out of questions before the clock ran out.    One of her mottos in life was, "Question Everything."    And if that motto were ever applicable, it would apply to ancient giants!    She was prepared...

A few hours later, Janice threw open the door of the building, with a wild look in her eye.  Where had time gone!  Her head was spinning from all the information she had just gleaned from this unassuming scientist slash academic.  One factoid after another just spilling from his lips.  Her hands were also full of some of his scientific papers he provided.

However, Janice could not afford to be late for Sean's business plus cocktails hour event.    It was the keystone event for this business trip, for it was the first time Sean's key customer relationship extended an invitation to an event at the family's home!  Surreptitiously, she kicked off her heels, stuffing them into her bag as she scurried across the emerald green lawn.  There was only one collegiate couple lolling in the grass oblivious to the barefooted Yankee in their midst.

Anxiously, she scanned the street for the town car and its driver that Linda seamlessly arranged.  Suddenly, Janice spied and hailed the driver, who appeared to be resting his eyes, as she was long overdue based on her provided ETA.  At that point, Janice let out a yelp, as she began hopping on one foot.  Sean teasingly called her a leather foot, which was true relative to him, but that only went so far. She forgot she was sprinting between oak trees. Acorns, twigs, and other deciduous matter were spread across her path. Hopping along on one foot, Janice wended her way and piled into the back seat. Checking her watch, she breathed a sigh of relief, she had thirty minutes before "kick-off".

Her cheerful driver accepted her apologies for being so late as she leaned back into the headrest. Janice began to mentally run through her wardrobe change ensuring that she could hit the number.

Sean often called her Shoehorn for shoving way too many things into one day. She had certainly earned the term of endearment. But this was also her obvious Achilles' Heel. This is when she really admired Sean's masculine trait of staying focused on the specific task. On the other hand, Janice practiced daily living with irons in many fires. She thought to herself, this is one of the reasons we work so well together. We come to the table with different strengths, but it could also get a little dicey at times.

When Janice exploded through the hotel room door, Sean was facing her buttoning up his tuxedo shirt, with these little fancy buttons that looked like playing cards. He was dressing in his usual methodical fashion, where he had on only his boxer shorts, socks and shoes and dress shirt.

The left-hand side of his face lifted slightly, both the corner of his lip and eyebrow. A questioning, welcoming yet skeptical smile that expressed with the use of no words exactly what her loving executive was thinking:

"What shenanigans had his wife stirred up now and how the hell was she going to pull off this Houdini act yet again?"

With a gush, Janice tore into the room kissing Sean full on the mouth as she peeled off clothes as she went. How was she going to explain what a fascinating rabbit hole she had fallen into today? There was a melting pot of academic arguments, politicians, big money, ethnic tensions, and archaeological power struggles. All of which would have to wait for a late-night meeting between the sheets, where she could pour into Sean's ear all the random threads of intel running through her mind.

As she turned on the shower to hot, no holds barred, Janice peeled the last layer of lingerie from her sweaty body as she ripped through her suitcase on the floor searching for her razor. She looked over at Sean's perfectly packed suitcase that appeared to have just arrived from Neiman Marcus replete with cellophane wrapped shirts.

"What a saint he was putting up with her insanity," she thought to herself.

Eight minutes later, after a few twists of her hair into a semblance of a French twist, she jammed her size 10 feet into her favorite pair of travel heels. They went with everything and were the perfect height for her already tall frame in both short to long dresses.

She was wearing a dress Sean had just given her, a picture of feminine versatility. It was cut on an asymmetrical bias, with the left side close to skimming the floor whereas the right was just above the knee. The background was cocktail party black, but shimmery. There was a subtle patchworking of tiny pink roses on the same black background randomly worked throughout the dress. Alluringly, one rosebud patch cupped her right breast while another runaway briar patch streaked away down her left thigh racing towards the floor. A symbolic study in motion perfectly appointed to the woman it adorned.

While searching for the hole in her earlobe with both hands, she turned to see Sean's broad swimmer-back facing her. He had found his tuxedo pants and was now completing his impeccable ensemble with her favorite pair of suspenders. They had the same emblematic pattern found on his buttons of the playing cards. She saw his thumbs pulling up his suspenders over those massive shoulders and time just stopped her.

Sean must have felt her stare as he turned to face her. With that enigmatic small smile he asked, "What?"

Startled Janice said, "What? Nothing! I am ready! See? Oh, ye of little faith," she attempted to inject a little humor into the twinge of tension in the air due to her late arrival.

Shortly thereafter, the intense couple was standing at what looked like a modest front door for Mr. Gervais, the CEO and Founder of Sean's important customer. The Gervais' were hosting a black-tie cocktail party for their daughter's engagement announcement. This was the main event that Sean had rearranged the timing of their trip to Columbia. For as Sean often noted, he was born in a little pee-wee town in the backwoods of South Carolina, but his Momma did not raise no fool. She taught him proper etiquette. When invited to formal family announcements, you went if you could help it.

By this time, Janice felt remorse for raising Sean's blood pressure due to showing up on the knife's edge of a minute. She promised herself to be on her best behavior at this Southern soiree which in and of itself raised her own Yankee anxiety a decibel or two.

As they waited at their hosts' entrance, Janice whispered what an enchanting modest home for such a Big Dog. With a small chuckle, Sean relaxed into his wife's tall frame, encircling her with his oar of an arm.

As Sean's hand slipped slightly down Janice's own back, he responded, "I forgot to tell you, we restrained Southern gentleman enjoy our Big in the Back." As the elegant glass French doors swung open, Janice did her best to stifle her giggles at Sean's humorous slide into double entendre.

Upon their arrival, they were led through the Gervais' lovely look-through living room with floor to ceiling windows framing the back wall. They overlooked a scaled terrace descending towards Lake Katherine stretched below their feet sparkling in the moonlight.

The Big was certainly in the back of this house. The spectacular panoramic view was quite breathtaking, especially when entering through the more modest front door.

As Janice followed Mrs. Gervais through the tour of her newly renovated kitchen admiring the unique granite selection, she paused to appreciate the warm hospitality she felt every time she visited Sean's home state. Her hostess began to fill in the blanks for Janice about all the French sounding names that were embedded into the fabric down here. A branch of the protestant Huguenots fled their French Catholic persecutors at the beginnings of America and were key settlers of South Carolina. The two women explored a theory they appeared to share: this historical French influence was part of the state's amazing spate of chefs and love for delicious food. And as is often the case, a commonly shared belief forms a new bond of friendship between otherwise unrelated parties.

For some reason, Janice enjoyed collecting random facts from storytellers, so she felt right at home. Mrs. Gervais was providing a brief history on the U.S. Corp of Army Engineers created the manmade Lake Katherine with dams during the 1940s. Something about getting a more sustainable water supply for the massive Army base positioned on the edge of town. Then something about a private owner taking management control naming the lake after his Mother. After the deluge of skeleton facts, Janice's listening skills were fading in and out, especially when sipping a Chablis who's minerality was reminiscent of the seashells found in its terroir.

As they continued their home tour, the ladies turned a corner and Janice stopped and stood stock still. She was shocked again for the second time on this action-packed day. The giant skeleton debriefing was massive in scope, but this was different. This shock was derived from the Divine's Synchronicity creeping into the edges of Janice's daily living and apparently beginning to set up residence.

Hanging directly in front of Janice's nose was the next piece in her art puzzle involving the unknown femme French Impressionist, J. Laurent! It was the elusive piece titled *Martius*.

Due to Ethan's largesse, Janette had access to the digital archives of Durand-Ruel's correspondence. Working together, they had deduced that the femme artiste had planned to complete a twelve-part series of these paintings that she dubbed her Calendar Series. Each piece was designed to evoke feelings, memories and inspiration related to a month of the year. So far, they surmised that she most certainly must have painted the first three works titled *Janus*, *Februus* and *Martius* each representing their respective month of January, February, or March.

But then something may have happened to her ambitious plans. There seemed to be an inference that her health was in question. Her father talked about Janette taking a "health cure" trip to the hot springs somewhere. Did she ever get to complete the rest of the months? And where were *Janus* and *Martius*? Sir Andrew Featherstone only had *Februus*.

Therefore, finding *Martius* serendipitously hanging in the hall of their gracious Southern hostess in the capital of South Carolina, was quite something. In fact, it briefly made Janice speechless, which Sean would say was quite the impossible task.

And in the way that only Janice could do, she had turned the business cocktail party on its head as it was now an art exhibition. Janice conferenced in Sir Andrew Featherstone and Ethan Pettit on their hostess' telephone.

The art collector was orally describing brushstrokes while Ethan was excitedly reading excerpts from the Durand-Ruel correspondence archive as supportive data points to their hostess. She was so enjoying the spotlight on one of her favorite pieces in her collection, while learning the trove of information of the mysterious unknown artist, Janette Laurent.

Outside circling the patio firepit, was a small cluster of the businessmen in attendance. Sean was enjoying scotch on the rocks in a big wine glass, his favorite way to imbibe that particular spirit. He did not really understand how others could drink scotch neat; it was way too intense for him that way. When others would question his scotch sensibilities, he would shrug his hulking shoulders in that mild way of his and say, "Well, I'm not a Scotsman, I'm an American, I like ice."

In a flurry of movement, he saw Janice charging towards him from the house. She was gesticulating wildly as she charged towards his group. Quickly, he hid the small smile playing across his lips, as Janice plowed into the male power pack. Oblivious to all, she was on her favorite mission of puzzling out unfathomable mysteries. God, Sean thought to himself, if only there were more built like her, they would have solved all the world's problems by now. But secretly he was glad that there was only one Janice, and they were pledged heart and soul to each other a long time ago.

After explaining her shocking find of Janette's *Martius*, the business of the evening was quickly forgotten as the party combined into one mass of humanity back inside. They surrounded the painting as the historical mystery spilled out from their lips and the telephone's speaker phone.

Later that evening, the vibrant couple was back in their hotel room winding down. Janice was rooting through the pack of papers strewn across the desk that Ethan had shared with her upon their departure from the Smithsonian. Thanks to Janice's filing methods, it was now a jumbled mix. The documents related to Janette's French paintings were now messily commingled into the majority. These were the printouts from the digital archives about the ancient giant skeletons found across North America in massive burial mounds.

One of the photocopies was of spidery handwriting, a flowing script from another time where people were taught cursive in school. It was a letter that caught her eye, as she did not recall seeing it before this moment. It started like this:

> *Dear Hackers of Humanity,*
> *We know what you did. You have hidden the evidence from us for a long time. You...*

Hackers of humanity? Who wrote this? When? But Sean was calling her from the bedroom. This intriguing missive must wait for another day.

Janice jumped up, flew into the bedroom, where she flung herself head first onto the bed into his waiting arms. He was laughing as hard as she was, for this pantomime was a code between them referencing their first night together.

That first magical evening, Janice had said she was falling head over heels for Sean and then tripped over her own two feet falling safely into his open arms. Without a hitch, Janice had then quipped, "Literally. Falling head over heels," which made them laugh all the harder.

Tonight, there were more important mysteries to be discovered in each other's arms. Ancient giant skeletons and a newly identified young French Impressionist were going to be set aside for the evening. They had been hidden in the annals of time for many years, they could wait a bit longer. The mysteries could be patient. For now, they had two sleuthing heroes ready and willing to shine the spotlight of truth on their mysterious secrets and share them with the world.

# DOWN RIVER BUT
# WITH A PADDLE

*38.9072° N, 77.0369° W*
*Journeying South... 2500s*

E m and Brave were completely alone now in the middle of a misty coastal river streaming South to Southwest. When they left the banks of The Island of the Lady, it was early morning. The dew was rising off the grassy riverbank surrounding the powerful form of the robed Februus. His pale face was mostly covered by the cowl of his robe.

As their canoe entered the hidden cross currents, Em's heart suffered a quick pang of sadness. It told her this would be the last time she would see Februus, her tribe and her island home. With regret, she thought about the fallen ancient relic of the A-mare-ikuns, the Lady of Liberty. Others must care for her now.

In her mind's eye, she saw Februus leaving his mortal body behind quite soon. He had made it clear that Brave and her mission was his last human project. In the flurry of planning their departure, all the little details seemed to get in the way. Em did not feel like they had the time to say a proper good-bye.

However, as they were stowing the last supplies into their canoe, there was one moment. Februus stilled her hands in one of his. He touched the middle of his own forehead with his thumb then lightly touched Em's forehead in the same place. Quickly he turned and performed the same small ritual with Brave.

Without one word being uttered, they were connected, the three of them. As an ancient writer had penned, a three strand cord is not easily broken. Diamonds seemed to be dancing in their minds' eyes. Somehow through that miraculous tangle of DNA that Februus introduced them to, they were all connected and communicating. They knew he would somehow remain in their minds and would help them access the wisdom within them when needed.

After a day or two on the waters, Brave steered their small craft into a small eddy. They could rest a bit and try to catch a few fish. That way they could save their salted meats for when food was scarce.

Em sat in the front of the canoe with her elongated back curving away from Brave. He was from the inner plains and was used to maneuvering in the small rivers near his home. He needed Em's intercoastal waterway expertise to navigate these foreign currents.

They made a perfect paddling pair in their punt. Brave's strength as the rudder in the back and Em's scouting eyes with the local pilot knowledge up front.

He could watch her forever Brave thought to himself. It was like watching a storm play out on the ocean's horizon. It was so intense but off in the distance, so you had no idea what was going on, until suddenly the storm was upon you.

However, now that Februus formed this new mind connection between them, Brave was realizing that physical distance was really a deception. They were both aware of each other's thoughts more and more each day. Especially out here on the water, there was something magical out there. It was a different energy then from walking on the land. The water seemed to transmit their thoughts more easily to each other.

A small smile crossed his lips as Em turned to face him in profile. With one glance, he was now feeling her thoughts again. They were starting to hold the same thought patterns. Based on her smile, it was apparent that she was reading his thoughts about her physical assets.

Shortly after, Em said, "Februus, wanted us to stop here for a bit. I need to show you some things."

Brave looked around at the endless bracken and bramble lining the river banks. He couldn't help but ask, "What? What do you mean here? This doesn't look any different from anywhere else we traveled. How do you know it is here?" He continued to peer into the swampy mists looking for some telltale landmark that Em had already spied with her eagle eyes.

Em cooly appraised him, clearly trying to gauge how to explain another inexplicable truth. Slowly, she raised a finger to the top of her head, and tapped it. She said,

"One of the skills of the Tribe of the Path is navigation. Many tribes lost this DNA activation, but we still have it. Did you ever think about why flocks of birds know where to fly when they migrate? How they will all turn together in unison? It is the same principle. We don't need landmarks, for we feel it in our heads. It is one reason we are called The Path."

As Brave was still digesting this, Em continued:
"While I was growing up, Februus taught me my lessons. One of my tasks was to learn the map of the Earth's globe in my head. When I was little it just felt like a fun game, I didn't know why I was learning this. He had a large orb that represented the whole planet. He would place my finger on different spots on the orb, then place his finger on top of my head. I would repeat the name of the location as I visually memorized its place. When he made the physical connection to my head, I could feel an electric charge. It was somehow programming each location into synchronicity with my brain."

Now Brave was speechless again, as if he was staring at a messenger straight from God. What else was going on inside of that head of hers? For that matter, what was going on in his own mind, that he didn't yet comprehend? He shook his shaggy locks to clear it again.

With an enigmatic nod, Em continued, "We are now about halfway to our destination in Carrow-Line-Ah. There we will find Martius, one of the remainingTwelve Elders. He will help us learn more about the ancient race of Mound Builders that were here before us little humans. Februus taught me that the Carrow-Line-Ahs was one of the Giants' important centers. A religious capital where they came and gathered. They were here who knows how many thousands of years ago."

"But right now we are currently in the A-Mare-ikun's capital that existed a few hundred years ago. They called it Wash-it-ton for their first leader. And also Col-um-bee-ah. Some of their leaders were very scared by the discovery of the race of the ancient giants. They did everything they could to hide this truth from the masses. So they sent their scientists around the country to collect the giant skeletons under the guise of academic study. But what did they do instead? They buried the bones in a massive secret vault right here under their nation's capital. I guess like conquerors do, they try to steal and use the energy of predecessors for their own ascent to more power.    And if they feel threatened by the powerful mysteries of the unexplained they bury it."

Quietly now, Em finished her unusually long monologue with:

"We only had the remains of that one giant skeleton on our Island of the Lady.    Here there are thousands and thousands in one massive underground crypt.    Februus added it to my brain map, so it will be easy for me to find.    It is time for us to camp so we can go explore it tomorrow."

This was the most Brave had ever heard Em verbally speak in the short spate of their relationship.  It was amazing information especially in light of the primitive lives they both led.  Survival was never easy here in the now.    Intuitively, Brave knew it was true, as he could feel it in her words.    He returned to the beautiful holographic image of the DNA strands rotating in his mind's eye again.    What else was stored in there?    And this was true for each human! What could they all achieve when accessing their own records? It was inspiring and overwhelming at the same time and it made their commitment to discovery both daunting and imperative.

As they stretched out near their campfire under a small rocky overhang, the young couple cuddled together under their snug animal skins.  They stared into the fire as their minds entwined together traveling into the murky historical past of humans and ancient giants.

As they drifted closer to the edges of slumber, they mentally discussed and agreed that:

These ancients must have been super powerful. If we are now learning how to access wisdom stored in our own DNA, perhaps that is what the scientists were after? Maybe they were trying to secretly extract DNA knowledge from the giants' bones to see what they could find for their own goals?

Even though they were new to their efforts of discovery, they were survivors of the remnant of humanity remaining on Earth. The one thing drilled into them by every adult was this: Beware of those that hoard wisdom and knowledge for their own ends. It will destroy.

They were taught that destruction had played out many times here on Earth. Power can corrupt the best of intentions. The last downfall included the unleashing of bioweapons of warfare against the masses by a few hoarders in some warped play for total control that then abruptly morphed into almost total annihilation of the human race.

The courageous pair knew that they were given several pieces already to a greater puzzle that would help humanity ascend yet again towards health and greater consciousness. Their limbs shivered more in recognition of their task than the cool night air as they curled deeper into each others' warmth. Em nestled further back under the cloak of Brave's arms wrapped around her as she fell into a deeper dreamy sleep.

Whatever surprises the days ahead might bring them, were suddenly less overwhelming. For the two soulmates, Shevanon and Jan-Waara had found each other again. They were now wearing the lives of Brave and Em walking a human timeline warped by corrupted negative outcomes. However, they were beginning to receive messages from their higher selves as well as from their past life experiences as Monsieur Durand-Ruel and the young Janette. Thirdly, there were more recent signals from their more modern lives as Sean and Janice.

Here they were together again in physical form, standing shoulder to shoulder. Yes they would face great adversity, but it was made easier via their mind and heart connections. Ties bound their souls together greater than ever before, as their human game played out again down in the miry clay on the great stage of humanity.

## ACKNOWLEDGEMENTS

My love to our two empathetic daughters, Hannah and Chloe, bravely forging their own paths. To my own Sweet Keith, my sacred haven. You are my daily Traveler's Rest when I return to recover from my mental excavations. To my fellow humans, we function best in unity when serving each other in loving gratitude as we live the dream of the Divine Cosmic Mind. Always look within. Onward we go!

## ABOUT THE AUTHOR

Erica Elliott is an artist at heart. She finds great joy in making art with her hands, whether that be with a pen, brush, fingers or a keyboard. She believes that ALL have the divine spark of creation shining inside, therefore she actively supports other Emerging Artists in their endeavors. Erica was brought up in a quite unorthodox yet loving household: friendly with Healers and finding purpose through communal connection. This upbringing allowed her to see people, circumstances and things in unusual ways. Her early memories were falling in love with words, drawing and numbers, all symbols that can point us along the mystical journey of life.

Visit the author online at

**EricaSwensonElliott.com**

## RECOMMENDED READING

*The Ancient Giants Who Ruled America* by Richard J. Dewhurst

*The Ancient Secret of the Flower of Life*, (Volumes 1 and 2) by Drunvalo Melchizedek

*America Before: The Key to Earth's Lost Civilization* by Graham Hancock

*The Brand Site: A Techno-Functional Study of a Dalton Site in Northeast Arkansa*s by Dr. Albert C. Goodyear

*Conversations with Nostradamus* (Volumes 1, 2, 3) by Dolores Cannon

*Cyberstorm: A Novel* by Matthew Mather

*Healing Mudras: Yoga for your Hands* by Sabrina Mesko

*Journey of Souls: Case Studies Between Lives* by Dr. Michael Newton

*Many Lives, Many Masters: The True Story of a Prominent Psychiatrist, His Young Patient and the Past-Life by Dr. Brian L. Weiss*

*Mysteries of Ancient America* by Fritz Zimmerman

*The Suppressed History of America:* by Paul Schrag and Xaviant Haze

*The Twelve Layers of DNA* (Kryon Book Twelve) by Lee Carroll

*Voyages of the Pyramid Builders* by Dr. Robert Schoch

*A Wrinkle in Time* by Madeleine L'Engle